Sam McBratney

During the last thirty years Sam McBratney has written many books for children of all ages. His work is known at home and abroad – international awards include the Abby (America), the Silveren Griffel (Holland) and the Bisto (Ireland). His picture book *Guess How Much I Love You* is one of the most successful books in the history of children's literature. Sam grew up in Lisburn, Northern Ireland, and still lives and works in County Antrim.

Also by SAM McBRATNEY

Funny, How the Magic Starts . . .
You Just Don't Listen

To Sydney, our oldest friend.

Contents

One grand sweet song
short stories

Sam McBratney

mammoth

First published in Great Britain in 1999 by Mammoth
an imprint of Egmont Children's Books Limited,
239 Kensington High Street, London W8 6SA

ISBN 0 7497 3835 9

10 9 8 7 6 5 4 3 2 1

A CIP catalogue record for this title is available from the British Library

Typeset by Avon Dataset Ltd, Bidford on Avon, B50 4JH
Printed in Great Britain by Cox & Wyman Ltd, Reading, Berkshire

CONTENTS

Be good, sweet maid, and let who will be clever;
Do noble things, not dream them, all day long,
And so make Life, and Death and that For Ever,
One grand sweet song.

Charles Kingsley

SWALK

Then come and kiss me, sweet-and-twenty,
Youth's a stuff will not endure.

William Shakespeare.

The card he was expecting arrived a day early. Monty Quayle found it waiting for him when he got home from school on 13th February. His first impulse was to chuck it on the fire and be done with it, for he had no time for this slushy, lovey-dovey St Valentine's Day nonsense; but he didn't do that. Perhaps the sheer size of the white envelope appealed to his sense of curiosity. It seemed far too big for his letter-box.

'Who's your admirer, then?' his mother asked slyly as she passed through the kitchen trailing coffee fumes.

'Some twit of a girl,' he said.

'In your form?'

1

'How do I know?' said Monty, heading smartly for the privacy of his own room. His mother had sneaked in two questions on this subject, and she'd had two answers – more than she had a right to expect.

Actually, he had a pretty good idea who was torturing him in this way. In yesterday's French class Gail Summers and Anne Clarke had informed him that he would be receiving a valentine card on 14th February.

'How do you know?' he'd asked in all innocence.

'A wee bird told us,' they said, adding that this card would have the French word for 'love' on it. *L'amour*, they said, shoving out their lips at him and kissing thin air until Anne Clarke laughed like a camel.

In the peace and quiet of his own room Monty examined the uninvited card with as much generosity of spirit as he could muster. One of the giant red hearts on the front had a jagged split running through it and it sickened him, that broken heart. Your heart was a thumping big muscle in the middle of your chest, it couldn't snap in two like a cheese and onion crisp and how people could ignore a simple fact like that was beyond his understanding. 'My heart longs for you', said one of the lines inside. Hearts couldn't long for anything, they were for pumping blood and you might as well long for somebody with your left kidney. 'My brain longs for you' would be better. Not that he wanted the brain of Anne Clarke to long for him, or that of Gail Summers either, but at least it would make sense from a biological point of view.

The whole card was a mass of scrawled verses which were so awful that he couldn't stop reading them. What could one say about:

Roses are red,

Violets are blue

If I had three feet

You'd be my third shoe?

A long stick of French bread had been drawn in one corner with a beret on its head. It also had legs. And sunglasses. *L'amour* said the heart-shaped bubble escaping from the mouth of this loaf.

Those two stupids were the guilty ones, all right.

On the reverse side of the envelope Monty noticed a word he had never seen before. It didn't even look English. S W A L K. What did that mean? Was it yet more French? Monty shoved the whole bundle of rubbish between the pages of an atlas.

Overnight the snow came down. The cars on every road took their time that morning. Although the pavements were awash with melting slush, you could still find the makings of a snowball on the tops of walls or lying on a hedge, and Monty found himself attacked by two people as he approached the school gates. Like most of the girls he knew, those two couldn't throw a snowball to save their lives.

'You missed,' he said.

'Did you get a valentine card this morning?' shouted Anne Clarke, snorting out steam like a dragon.

'No I didn't, so hard cheese.'

'Well, we know somebody who sent you one, don't we, Gail?'

'Did you send it?'

'Us?' screeched Anne Clarke. 'What makes you think it was *us*?'

Monty did not understand this behaviour, so he went into school hoping that his friend Conor would be back after his dose of the 'flu.

During the morning he made a point of standing at the back of every line, a tactic which allowed him to go into each classroom last and so avoid Anne Clarke and Gail Summers. If he went in first, they might sit down beside him. Conor couldn't understand why he wasn't pushing and shoving for a radiator seat like everybody else.

In French he put up his hand and asked, quietly, 'Miss Peters, is "swalk" a French word?'

She peered at him through the rainbow-framed glasses on the bridge of her nose. She didn't have to peer far, for Monty's tactics had forced him to take a seat at the front of the room. Under her nose, in fact.

'What?'

'The word "swalk", Miss – is it French?'

'Spell it.'

'S-W-A-L-K.'

Some tittering from behind made him wonder whether he had asked an intelligent question.

'Are you trying to be funny, Monty Quayle?' said Miss Peters icily, then went on to describe the peculiar habits of some French verb, leaving unsolved the mystery of 'swalk'.

According to a powerful rumour which invaded the school at lunch-time, all the teachers were afraid of being snowed in and the place was closing early; but that didn't happen. As Conor and Monty walked home at the usual time, Conor – imitating Miss Peters – said, 'Are you trying to be funny, Monty Quayle?' Millions of his 'flu germs were spluttered over the slushy grey snow. 'I nearly wet myself when you asked her about "swalk".'

Monty just smiled, as if being a wonderful wit came naturally to him.

'You didn't get a valentine card?' Conor asked shrewdly – a little dart of a question.

'You must be kidding,' said Monty. 'Me? Valentine card?'

When he got home it was to find that a second card had been delivered to his house, by hand, without a stamp, simply pushed through his front door without so much as a by-your-leave. Monty saw no reason why that sort of thing should be legal.

'Is it from the same person?' his mother wanted to know as she hovered there.

'I don't know,' said Monty, staring at the two words written in capitals on the flap. SWALK and SWALK. Two of them. Plural swalks.

'What does "swalk" actually mean?' he asked, making use of his mother.

'Sealed with a loving kiss.'

'Cut out the goo talk, Mum.'

'It does. Goo talk, indeed! S for sealed, W for with, L for loving, K for kiss. It's short for sealed with a loving kiss.'

Hell's bells! And he'd asked Miss Peters, who now thought of him as a fool, if it was French – she'd think he was girl-mad. Sealed with a loving kiss! Oh, the shame of it, and he hated kissing: his relatives no longer tried it on because he'd put a stop to it – on TV he hated that cissy lip stuff and the horrible sucking noises made by people joined together at their mouths! The humiliation he felt was colossal – his pride all drained away.

He threw the valentine card on the fire and watched until both SWALKs were consumed by it utterly.

'Well, that's not a very nice way to get on,' his mother said. Not that he cared. She had no understanding of the situation whatsoever.

I'll send *them* a card! Monty raved upstairs. I'll send them some card, all right, and it'll be plastered with words the French never heard of. SWAFEJ, he thought. Sealed with a frog's eyeball juice. And SWAMS. Sealed with a monkey's stink. In no time at all he had a dozen good ones – letters with acid rain, elephant's wee-wee, a pelican's egg yolk, lubricating oil, mashed maggots and worse. Much worse. This line of thinking was effective in its own way, for he had calmed down quite a lot by the time he looked out of his bedroom and saw both of them standing in the street below.

They had a spaniel-looking dog lolloping round their legs. The sight of this thing's floppy ears and its big soft belly as round as a melon inspired Monty with a cunning idea. Down the stairs he flew, three at a time, calling out for Crazy Wolf to appear at his side.

Their yappy dog had actually been named Patch for an obvious reason, but he also answered to names like Fleabag, Muttface and Crazy Wolf. That dog hated every living thing that did not belong to its own family; and it hated, besides, non-living things within the family. The Hoover was its mortal enemy. If you held up a mirror he also went berserk, which meant that Crazy Wolf was a creature who even hated himself. Monty opened the door just enough – and let him loose. Some people were about to learn that it didn't pay to lurk.

This plan backfired horribly, as Monty had to admit when he sneaked down the path some moments later. His fool of a dog was actually showing off in front of the spaniel with a display of athletic twirls and frisky jumps. In between the jumps and twirls there occurred some rubbing of noses. Swalk, thought Monty – bitterly – again. It was as if the creature knew it was St Valentine's Day.

'Your dog likes Sheila,' said Anne Clarke.

'He's just friendly,' lied Monty, scooping up the animal into his arms. This was to stop the disgusting smelling of behinds that was now going on.

'Did you get a valentine card?'

'Yes I did.' He was flustered, and could not duck the question.

'We know who sent it even though there's no name on it, don't we, Gail?'

Gail Summers blushed until her cheeks glowed; and then the beast within the cradle of Monty's arms began to whine with desire. A stump of a tail flicked backwards and forwards in front of his face like a windscreen wiper.

'It wants its tea,' Monty explained, retreating up the path and into the house again, where Crazy Wolf got told in no uncertain terms what a big soft wet pudding he had degenerated into.

About the same time on the following day there came a knock at the front door which Monty, to his regret, left his mother to answer.

She returned saying, 'It's young Gail Summers. She wants to know is your dog coming out? And you needn't look at me like that – go and speak to her.'

There she stood on his step, with spaniel, wearing a woollen hat and a scarf that seemed to go round her neck at least three times. Not much of her face could be seen.

'Is Patch coming out?' she asked.

Patch, he thought. And how did she get to know Fleabag's real name? Had she been making enquiries?

'He's got a thorn in his foot.'

'Is it sore?'

'We had to bathe it.'

'I'm sure he squealed.'

'Yes,' said Monty. This was all lies, but he had no choice and did not blame himself.

'Did you use disinfectant?'

'And cream,' he said, holding on to the door in case Crazy Wolf put in an appearance.

'Well, bye-bye, then,' said Gail, with a twist at Sheila Spaniel's lead. 'I'll see you in school tomorrow.'

'Goodbye,' said Monty, as if he was leaving that night for Australia.

This business about the valentine cards forced him to take a look at himself in the long mirror that evening, and to ask: what could there be about that person on the other side of the looking-glass to compel someone to send him a card that was sealed not once, but twice, with a loving kiss? Surely such magnetism in a human being would be obvious and recognisable? All the same, he couldn't find it.

After viewing himself from many angles he remained none the wiser.

Going to school next day he noticed Gail Summers on the road ahead of him. It was a treacherous morning for walkers, and ridges of frozen slush glinted in the early sunlight, but Monty knew that she was not walking slowly on account of the ice. The idea was that he should catch up with her, which he did.

'Daddy had to break the ice on our pond this morning,' she said.

'Goldfish?' he said.

'No, it's for wildlife. We get water beetles and tadpoles in the spring. Goldfish eat tadpoles. One slurp and they're gone.'

'My girlfriend has goldfish,' Monty suddenly blurted out. 'They're big ones, as long as your foot, I'd say.'

'Who is she?'

The cheek of this question – the colossal amount of sheer nosiness involved in it – allowed Monty to stare at her angrily.

'It's none of your business who she is.'

'You haven't got one, that's why.'

'That's where you're wrong.'

'Well who is she, then?'

She didn't believe him! In spite of the fact that he had even described his girlfriend's goldfish, his word was not good enough for her!

'She's Glenda Finch, if you must know.'

Glenda was a rough sort, the sort who pulled hair and who wouldn't take kindly to anyone who tried to steal her boyfriend. On the spur of the moment she was a very good choice, Monty was thinking. As he parted company with Gail Summers he felt that he had solved his problem, for anybody with any sense would now find another person to pursue.

At break-time Conor told him that Glenda Finch was looking for him.

'What for?'

'Dunno,' said Conor. 'Something to do with rumours and goldfish. She says you're saying things about her and she's going to squash you like a grub. You know what she's like, Glenda.'

Oh no. Only too *well*, he knew what Glenda was like. No matter which point of the compass she approached from you heard her coming, and you heard her go. She went through life making mountains out of molehills and molehills out of mountains.

Rather like a mole himself, Monty went underground for the rest of the morning. Great care had to be taken while crossing the playground, and he longed for a periscope to enable him to see round corners and down corridors. Often he reflected on the treachery of girls like Gail Summers, who could send you a letter sealed with a loving kiss on Tuesday and then land you right in it the day after.

From a person such as Glenda Finch there could be no hiding place, of course. She trapped him in the lunch-room. There was, in fact, an open window, but only a genuine coward could have done a bunk like that, and anyway, she spotted him first.

'You're saying things about me, Monty Quayle! You said I'm your *girlfriend*!'

The whole situation – he saw as one detached – was completely crazy. People stopped chewing to watch and hear the spectacle. And the craziest thing of all was that yes, somehow he had said that. My girlfriend is Glenda Finch, he'd said. And why? He must have been temporarily off his head. Glenda could never be anyone's girlfriend, for crying out loud, it would be too dangerous.

'And you said I sent you a valentine card! You'd better watch it, Quayle, I wouldn't send you a valentine card for a pension and I wouldn't be your girlfriend if you were the last person left alive after a nuclear bomb, you skinny wee shrimp. And I haven't got *goldfish*!' she screamed, finishing on a high note. Monty wondered desperately if he could pretend that there was another Glenda Finch.

There was more. Monty fought back with such statements as 'Shut your spout, fat whale' in order to avoid being overwhelmed completely. After the contest he felt quite tingly and invigorated – as joggers must do, he reflected.

And Gail Summers did not trouble him again from that time on.

The days raced by, and the long evenings of summer came again. That was the year when the Quayle family went abroad for the first time on a camping holiday in Northern France. Part of the thinking behind the holiday was that Monty would get a chance to practise his French, but he spent the time playing with English children and got by with a few French words for sweets. While they were away Crazy Wolf attacked a moving Volkswagen in the street and banjoed his leg. The mutt recovered all right but, once arthritis set into his left hip, he could hardly muster the enthusiasm to see off a stray cat.

Two more summers went by. Monty found himself looking up at the sky at night, and wondered about the distances between the stars, and who, if anyone, had created space on such a monumental scale – and why? These thoughts were new to him. They made him sense for the first time the amazing brevity of life on earth, including his own. On some occasions he experienced in the evenings what he himself described as 'the coloured peace of sunsets'; on others, he felt disturbed by vague longings which he could not name. He grew conscious of his appearance and cared especially for his hair. The thought of going thin on top like his dad scared the wits out of him.

The girl he fancied was Gail Summers. Wherever he went he carried in his mind's eye the fling of her dark hair and the swaying of her body – these were things he could not forget, and to hear her laughing in the company of other people was like hearing laughter over the wall of a scented garden from which a time warp had excluded him. In his heart – figuratively speaking, of course – he conceded that if he had three feet she'd be his third shoe: but she was now going strong with some fellow from Bell's Hill.

O, call back yesterday, bid time return.

William Shakespeare.

Gypsy

Now is the time for the burning of the leaves.

Laurence Binyon.

Gypsy came into the house before Danny Murray was born. She hung on the wall above the battered old piano with the yellow keys. Danny didn't like her cross face when he was little. Sometimes when he did his piano practice he climbed up on the stool and turned the picture to the wall so that she couldn't listen.

Gypsy had thin red lips under a crooked big nose. Her eyelids were always half-closed in a sly sort of way – as if to hide what she was really thinking. The pearls round her neck looked like blobs of paint from close-up, but when you stepped back they caught the light, and glowed. Like magic, really. Gypsy was so real that Danny used to wonder whether she was still alive somewhere in the world.

One day Catherine Parr from down the street came into the house and said that Gypsy's lips were red because she ate poisonous berries. She stuck out her tongue at Gypsy and she made Danny do the same.

When Danny was nine Gypsy got him into trouble. He climbed up on the piano stool and tried to give her a shave with his daddy's razor and wobbling brush, but his mother came into the room at the wrong moment, and caught him in the act.

'Oh, my glory!' she said. Mountains of creamy lather stood out from Gypsy's chin like snow-capped mountains on a map of the world. An avalanche of snow had blocked up her long, crooked nose.

'Danny Murray! Oh, I will murder you, you bad article. Brian – come you in here this minute, he's shaving *Gypsy*!'

His daddy arrived, breathless, and did some staring at Gypsy's altered face.

'What are you playing at? Are you stupid? There hangs the one thing in the house that could be worth a fortune, and what do *you* do with it? Give it a blasted *shave*!'

And so Danny found himself driven up the stairs by the flat of his father's hand. That was the first time he realised that Gypsy might not be just any old picture. In some mysterious way, maybe she was worth something.

About this time Dr Moore began to call at the house to examine Danny's father, who wasn't feeling well. During one of these visits the doctor happened to notice Gypsy.

'Mrs Murray,' he said, peering through his bushy eyebrows, 'I have to remark on that dark-skinned beauty on your wall. Now that's what

I call a proper picture! Where did you get her – did you pick her up at one of these fancy auctions?'

'No sure we've had that for years,' said Danny's mother. 'Maggie O'Brien and her man lit out for Canada and they sold all their stuff at the front door. My grandfather bought the picture and her mangle for two and six.'

Dr Moore smiled, and repeated, 'Two and six!' as he turned the painting over in his hands. 'Pity it's not signed. But look at the canvas. I'd say this wasn't done by one of your weekend artists. Did you ever think of selling it?'

'Ah no,' said his mother, going a bit red. 'Brian says we couldn't sell our luck.'

'Well now – give me the first refusal,' said Dr Moore, who aimed a massive wink at Danny as he put his stethoscope on Gypsy's chest and pretended to be deafened by the noise of her insides.

After that, Danny's parents talked about Gypsy as if she was money in the bank. His daddy used to say that he was going to sell Gypsy and buy a yacht and keep it in the harbour at Ballyholme. His mother wanted a house in the country with chickens and a goat. 'How Will We Spend Gypsy?' became a favourite family game. Then, when Danny turned eleven, his father died and, of course, everything changed.

For a long time Danny didn't know what to feel. He had tried to be like his daddy. He'd always been pleased when people said, 'That child's image of his father', and he didn't like the people who said he took after his mother. Something within him had died. He saw that

15

he had loved his daddy, but had not known this. Not really, not until now. And of course the knowing was part of his pain.

The Headmaster said special prayers for Danny in Assembly one morning. People were sorry for him because his daddy had gone away to heaven and, indeed, he was sorry for himself and for his mummy. It was a long time before she did many of her ordinary things about the house, such as play the old piano in the living-room. Then one day she played and made Danny sing that stupid song about Paddy McGinty's goat, and Danny felt good. They bought a black labrador pup and they had trouble teaching it not to widdle everywhere.

Danny noticed another change that came over his life at this time: there was no money to spend now that they had to live on what his mummy earned. Sometimes he remembered the day when he bought three bars of Fruit and Nut in the sweet shop and ate them one after another on the way to school.

'You are one greedy spoiled pig, Danny Murray,' Catherine Parr had told him, just because he only gave her two squares.

Now, times had changed. Catherine Parr was able to go on the school trip to Brittany, but Danny's mother sat down and cried when he told her what it would cost.

'I didn't want to go anyway,' Danny told her.

Even when his mother became manageress of the laundry where she worked on the Newtownards Road, still she complained that he grew too fast and ranted about the awful things he could do to a pair of shoes.

'I am going to buy you a pair of wooden Dutch clogs, Danny Murray,' she used to say.

His mother was great friends with the woman who owned the local fruit and vegetable shop. This lady, Miss Foster, gave Danny a job after school on Fridays and all day Saturdays. He spent most of the time sweeping the floors and making up delivery boxes. One afternoon Danny was wrapping an old newspaper round six big earthy leeks when an interesting headline caught his eye:

Fortune in Attic

A County Antrim farmer learned yesterday that the painting found in his attic could be worth as much as £80,000.

'I'm only flabbergasted,' he told our reporter. 'It's been up there for years. I nearly threw it out. I don't even like it, you know – I like pictures with horses in them.'

When asked what he was going to do with his unexpected windfall, Mr Cowan said, 'Enjoy it!'

Danny began to think. If his mummy had eighty thousand pounds she wouldn't have to scrimp and save or worry about the price of shoes. He thought of Gypsy's sly, hooded eyes; of the fine, strong jaw he'd once tried to shave; of the pearls round her neck and how they seemed to glow from within if the light was right. Only a good artist could paint like that, even Dr Moore had said so.

How much, he wondered, was Gypsy really worth?

'Dan Murray,' called Miss Foster from the front of the shop. 'What's keeping those leeks – are you growing them, or what?'

That very evening, Danny made a point of sitting with his mother while she did some ironing. From time to time she wet the clothes with vapour from a plastic spray.

'Mummy?'

'U-huh?'

'Miss Foster says if you take a picture into a shop near the City Hall, they'll tell you what it's worth.'

'Is that a fact, Danny?'

'What would you buy if we sold Gypsy?'

For a moment or two, no answer came. His mother squeezed a squirt of misty water over the collar of a shirt.

'I couldn't sell Gypsy, I've had her since I was a wee girl.'

'But if you *did* sell her, what would you buy?'

'A cuckoo clock!' said his mother, aiming a squirt of water at him. 'Now run away out and play.'

Two more weeks went by, bringing the end of term and the start of the Easter holidays. Danny was bored in the house on his own. Most of his best friends were away with the school to Brittany and it didn't help him to think what a great time they must all be having over there. On Tuesday afternoon he came back from walking the dog in the Ormeau Park, and made a decision that made his blood race.

He gently lifted Gypsy from the wall, put her into a large carrier bag, and caught a bus into town.

18

The journey into the centre of Belfast seemed to take about two minutes, for Danny's mind would not be still when he thought of what might happen in the next half hour. Goodbye Mr Scrimp and Mr Save. His mother might even give up her job! They could both fly out to see Uncle Robert in New Zealand or buy a house in the country and keep chickens and a car. Danny could think of a dozen ways of spending Gypsy, even if she wasn't worth quite as much as eighty thousand pounds.

He walked down Wellington Place and stood outside the shop with his heart beating like an engine, urging him on. His blood quickened, but his mind refused to be driven and he could not move. His mother would have a fit if she saw him right now! Danny closed his eyes and swallowed, thinking nervously how this was a bit like getting into the cold sea at Millisle. He took the plunge and went right in.

He was the only customer in the cool and very quiet gallery. The central area of the shop was fairly dim compared with the walls, which were illuminated by strips of fluorescent lighting. Some of the pictures hanging there were so huge that they made Gypsy look like a puny little thing – and to his amazement, Danny saw some very fancy carpets hanging on the walls. Funny place to keep your carpets, he was thinking when a voice spoke.

'Yes? What do you want?'

The man who now approached wore a shabby Aran jumper. Using his fingers as a comb, he shifted his long grey hair away from his face.

'I've got a picture here,' said Danny. 'Could you tell me, please, if it's worth anything?'

'Another one. All right, let's take a look at it.'

The man fitted glasses over his nose as he carried Gypsy a little closer to the window. He tapped the canvas with a fingernail and turned her over to examine the back just as Dr Moore had done all those years ago. Danny wanted to tell him some interesting things about his picture – how her name was Gypsy, that they'd had her for years and years, how she was supposed to be lucky – but he didn't have time. The man whipped the glasses off his face.

'This painting has no commercial value whatsoever. The frame might fetch a penny or two if it was competently restored, but the work itself . . . ? Most likely a student's copy. No.'

Danny took back his picture without speaking. No commercial value. A copy. That final word fell on his ears like a blow – No. He swallowed hard, gathering his courage, wanting to strike back.

'But . . . didn't you see her pearls?'

'I saw her pearls.'

Gypsy! How it destroyed him to think she wasn't even worth a cuckoo clock.

'But how do you *know*? How do you know she isn't worth anything?'

'Look, son,' said the man. 'What's your name?'

'Danny Murray.'

'Right. Suppose that twenty or thirty women lined up outside this shop and one of them was your mother. And suppose they all shouted, "Danny Murray!" one after another. Do you think you'd know your mother's voice, could you pick it out from all the others?'

'Probably.'

'Well that's how it is with paintings. You know your mother's voice when you hear it because you're an expert on that topic. A great and valuable painting is like an old friend – an expert like me can pick it out immediately. Now go home, and take that Gypsy with you. A painting doesn't have to be worth money to be valuable.'

Away he went into a far corner of his shop leaving Danny to shove Gypsy into the carrier bag any old way, as if he was ashamed of her now that she was just plain cheap, and angry with her for making a fool out of him.

I hate that man! he thought as he crossed the road at Bedford Street lights. I hate him and his stupid shop and I hate his stupid carpets on his stupid walls.

How Will You Spend Gypsy? The game was over. Perhaps his mother had known all along. And Dr Moore. His daddy, too. Maybe I was the only one who believed in Gypsy, thought Danny. The whole business filled him with such a deep, vague sadness that he wanted to be very, very young again.

When he got home his mother said, 'And where have you been to, my lad? And just be careful what you say because I think I know.'

'Mummy, I just took it into that shop.'

'Did you! Well you had no business taking it anywhere, give it to me, here.'

She examined the picture for signs of damage, and seemed satisfied. 'And what did they say in that shop?'

'I didn't go in,' Danny said quickly. 'I hadn't the nerve. Well, it was a big shop.'

All of a sudden his mother giggled, and gave him a peck on the cheek. 'Ah, dear love you, sure you're only young.'

She fitted the picture over the lighter patch of wallpaper that marked the spot, and said, 'There you are now, Gypsy,' as if things were more or less back to normal.

Time is the great physician.

Disraeli.

The Electric Rejuvenator

Sweet childish days, that were as long as twenty days are now.

William Wordsworth.

When I was in my early teens I used to spend my holidays with Aunty Eileen and Uncle Joe, who lived in a high terraced house near Donaghadee.

Those were lovely days and I remember them so well. I had a boyfriend whose dad set lobster pots out at sea. From my window in the roof I could look across the bay to the little white lighthouse, where the young boys and the men fished all day from the pier. They seemed so patient waiting for their bites, and yet so silly. I didn't know any women who wasted time like that. After dark the beam from the lighthouse flashed through my attic room, and it was wonderful to fall asleep listening to the ocean. But what I remember most about Donaghadee is Uncle Joe's Electric Rejuvenator.

At that time my Uncle Joe was a tall and very bony-looking man in his forties. He would sometimes shave at the kitchen mirror, his braces dangling loose as he concentrated mightily on each stroke with a cut-throat razor. I was fascinated by the hollows behind his collar bones. They were so deep that they looked spooky to me. The boniest part of him was his round bald skull, which came out in freckles if he got the sun.

Uncle Joe suffered badly from a curious thing called hypochondria. Until I was thirteen or so I thought this was a kind of snake but as far as I know it doesn't occur among animals at all. It affects some grown-ups. They think they're ill when they're not. My Uncle Joe was the first hypochondriac I ever knew.

In the beginning I believed him when he said there was something the matter with him because I didn't know any better, and a man who can come out with hair-raising words like aneurisms, duodenums, ducts and bile seemed to know what he was talking about.

One day, as we brushed the lino on the stairs, I asked Aunty Eileen if Uncle Joe really *was* sick. She made a sharp little 'tch, tch' sound with her tongue, then whisked me into their bedroom on the middle floor. Opening a drawer lined with wallpaper, she showed me a selection of Uncle Joe's medicines – boxes of pills, liquids in coloured bottles, tubes of ointment and one or two fearful gadgets. The drawer gave off an odour of Wintergreen, or some such rub for sore backs.

'There you are,' said Aunty Eileen. 'He takes some of this stuff every blessed day in life! I don't know, it's like a chemist's shop.'

'But what exactly is the matter with him, Aunty Eileen?' I asked.

'Everything, love. You name it, he's got it.'

'Well he doesn't look sick,' I said. 'Just a bit thin.'

'Don't I know rightly, that's the whole point! It's all in his head, dear.'

We finished brushing the middle flight of stairs. Aunty Eileen flicked a small pile of dust on to a card I was holding, and after a glance down the hall, began to speak quietly.

'Listen, don't let him worry you with his talk. Your Uncle Joe tried to join the army when the war started but the army wouldn't have him. It was the medical, you see, they said something inside him was murmuring. Well, the shock *that* gave him started him on pills and he's been taking them ever since like sweets.'

'And *was* there something murmuring inside him?'

'Oh I dare say. Nerves, probably.' She giggled and pinched my cheek and told me to pay no attention to him. 'Not to worry, pet. He's still in the land of the living.'

She was adorable, my Aunty Eileen, and I loved her for so many reasons. The silliest reason is that when I was seven she taught me how to say the name of the plant *gypsophila-paniculata-compacta*. For ages I was certain that only two people in the world knew how to say that word: Aunty Eileen was one and I was the other. She was a rounded, cheerful, willing workhorse of the kind who passed into history with iron stair-rods and horseshoe mangles. She used to saw wood, get the coal, do the cooking and fetch and carry shopping, while Uncle Joe nursed some pain or other on the sofa. I helped her with painting and decorating in the summertime, and she was so grateful for my efforts, and so free with her praise, that I glowed with the joy of feeling grown up.

One Friday Uncle Joe arrived home with the news that his foreman had died suddenly. Since Uncle Joe never missed a funeral, Aunty Eileen decided that his good suit could do with a press. As we were taking it out of the wardrobe she noticed a newspaper cutting tucked away in his bowler hat, which also contained a pair of kid gloves and a folded orange sash. The bold print of the cutting read:

Feel young again.
Astonish your friends with your vitality.
Send now for the **Richardson, Smyth and Styles Electric Rejuvenator** (patent pending)

'An electric rejuvenator,' whispered Aunty Eileen. 'What in the name of glory could that be?'

I said I didn't know.

'Well go on, read me the small print.'

So I did. The Richardson, Smyth and Styles Electric Rejuvenator (patent pending) was a marvellous instrument, completely new to the market and recently invented by top doctors and scientists. It claimed to clean your blood, tone up your muscles and fine-tune your nervous system. If I remember correctly, it guaranteed you everything but a third set of teeth. For further information you were to write to an address in England. The advertisement also carried a quote from a satisfied customer, who claimed that his whole body was now 'humming with life' after using the Electric Rejuvenator for only one week.

Aunty Eileen listened to all this, sighed, and finally pushed the cutting into the crown of the bowler hat. 'Oh I don't know,' she muttered, shaking her head. 'It sounds like some daft machine. We'll just put it back and pass no remarks, dear.'

A few days later Aunty Eileen went into town while Uncle Joe and I weeded the front garden. To be more exact, I did the weeding while he sat on the front step smoking a cigarette. A fit of coughing suddenly bent him double, turning his face and neck scarlet. Solemnly he wagged the cigarette at me, scattering ash.

'These things are killing me, you know.'

He stubbed it out. Soon, I knew, he would light up another.

'You'd better not smoke when you grow up,' he said.

'Why not?'

'Because I'll be cross, that's why. Very cross. Anyway, it's not nice for girls to smoke.'

'I won't be a girl when I grow up, I'll be a lady.' Uncle Joe brought out the worst in me.

'Same thing! Some day you might be running for a bus and you might not catch it because you have no breath, and you might miss the bus.'

'I'll wait for the next one,' I said.

'For an hour and a half? Huh, some wait!'

The postman arrived, thank goodness. He came up the garden path with the biggest parcel I had ever seen and set it down in the hall. Someone had taken the time to coat all the knots in the string with red wax.

'It's come from Wolverhampton,' I said.

'Give it here,' said Uncle Joe rather gruffly.

I beseeched him with a look to open it there and then, but he disappeared up the stairs without saying a word. The parcel tinkled as he lugged it up and I almost wished that it was broken. Half an hour later he ventured into the kitchen as I peeled the potatoes. He patted me on the curls.

'By the way, child, be a good girl for your Uncle Joe and don't mention that parcel to your Aunty Eileen.'

'Why, what's in it?'

'It's scientific, you wouldn't understand.'

'We do science in school,' I said. 'Is it a surprise?'

'Ah . . . Yes. Yes. It's a surprise.'

It was no such thing. It was a secret. Uncle Joe never intended that anyone should find out what was in that parcel – but we did find out. A meeting in the church hall was cancelled one evening because the flower arranger missed her train, and Aunty Eileen and I arrived home to find Uncle Joe sitting in his underpants on the parlour rug, wired up.

He had electrodes attached to his big toes. His shoulders fitted neatly into a pair of metal epaulettes, each with its oscillating antenna. The various wires of the Rejuvenator converged within a black control box, which in turn plugged my Uncle Joe into the national grid. On his head he wore a little silver cap about the size of a saucer, presumably to ensure that the current passed right through him. And this whole fantastic apparatus quietly hummed, so that he wanted only a pair of wings to pass himself off as the world's most incredible insect.

My Aunty Eileen said, 'Oh my God!'

At first we wondered if he was alive at all, for he held himself very stiffly. Then the eyeballs moved and a thin arm snaked out towards the cigarette in the ashtray on the floor.

'Are you all right?' Aunty Eileen barked at him.

'Certainly I'm all right. Can't you see I'm all right?'

'What is that?'

'What?'

'You know fine rightly what! That . . . that *thing* you're sitting in. Is there something wrong with your toes?'

'No, it's for all of me. It gives you new youth.'

'New youth? New youth?' said Aunty Eileen, now edging her way round the room with her back to the wall, as if she wasn't entirely safe in the same space as the Electric Rejuvenator. I read her mind, and put on the kettle for a cup of tea.

She sank into a kitchen chair. 'Bless you, pet. To think I nearly invited Lizzie Wilson back for a bite of supper! Imagine her seeing a sight like that, he's like something from Mars. Oh good glory, new youth!'

And with that she rose up to rummage wildly in a drawer until she found a screwdriver. Holding this high above her head she raced to the parlour door, shouting, 'You see that? That's what you need.'

'What for?' I heard.

'For the screw that's loose inside your stupid head, Joe Wright.'

'My screws aren't loose,' said Uncle Joe huffily. 'What do you know about these things, anyway? I knew you'd get on like that.' And he wouldn't come out of the Electric Rejuvenator for twenty minutes more.

All the same, that was the end of it. One day when he was at work, Aunty Eileen gave the Rejuvenator to the binmen in case he fried himself. One of the binmen asked her what it was and she told him it was a television aerial that didn't work.

I am tempted to write that the Richardson, Smyth and Styles Electric Rejuvenator did not work, either – that it failed to rejuvenate. To be fair, though, I have to say that my Uncle Joe is still very much alive and kicking. Some years ago he took early retirement, convinced that he had only a few months left in him.

My Aunty Eileen went and died first, she who never had worse than a headache. I remember her so well, which is a tribute, I suppose, to the magic of memory and the significance of time. It's as if the cursor of my mind can click on the word 'Donaghadee' and there she is, dear love her, with the lighthouse flashing in the dark, the dulce blackening on the harbour wall, the ocean beating its own measure of time, and the proud saying-out-loud of *gypsophila-paniculata-compacta*. Uncle Joe was heartbroken, for he had been devoted to her in his peculiar, dependent way. It came as no surprise when he sold the house to buy a bungalow. Those three flights of stairs had preyed on his mind for years.

I still see him occasionally. During our last encounter (I noticed that he'd switched to cork-tipped cigarettes at last) he glared at my teenage daughters and warned them both to work hard for their exams. 'A bit of hard work never hurt anybody,' he said, and then gravely informed me that he had spinal arthritis.

'Uncle Joe,' I said. 'If you had spinal arthritis you wouldn't be up and about, would you?'

'Ah,' said he, 'but I'm seein' a specialist.'

And with that away he went, hobbling past the shops in Royal Avenue, acting on the same principle which has governed him since they heard that murmur inside him long ago: if you've got an illness, you flaunt it.

But at my back I always hear
Time's wingèd chariot hurrying near.

Andrew Marvell.

Aristocrockery

Thou art thy mother's glass, and she in thee
Calls back the lovely April of her prime.

William Shakespeare.

As soon as Michael asked her to go to the rugby club ball, Lynn knew her mother was the one she had to convince. 'You want to go to a formal dance? And you're not even seventeen? Well I don't know about that. What does your father say?'

Her elder brother Gordon laughed his awful oafish laugh again and her father said, 'I suppose she's got to get used to the ways of the world sooner or later.'

'Let it be later, then,' replied her mother. 'The ways of the world are soon enough got used to when she's left school.'

From then on, it was a matter of being especially helpful about the house, and of being tactful in her answers to a multitude of questions about the coming event. Who was he anyway? She wanted to know. A rugby player! They were the worst kind. Did she know his people? No, so he could be anybody. What age was he? Eighteen! They'd no sense at eighteen, especially if he was a student? Yes, she thought so, and with a flat of his own, no doubt. And did he smoke, did he drive, and did she go into pubs with him when they were out together?

It was alcohol that bothered her mother most, so Lynn was very careful with her answer.

'Look, Mummy,' she said patiently. 'He drinks very little – he has to play rugby. If it's drink you want to see, go down to the disco where it isn't even on sale. Half of them are full to the eyeballs and you don't make a fuss about me going there.'

'No, but you're not with anybody in particular.'

'What does that mean?'

'It means you're with girlfriends, not dancing with one boy the whole night. I don't like to think of you dancing with one person all the night long, it's too serious.'

But Lynn managed to swing the argument her way in the end. It helped when she admitted that she wasn't all that keen on Michael anyway, it was more the occasion she was going for.

On the night of the dance she was picked up at her front door by the eighteen-year-old rugby player who shook hands with her parents and promised to have her back on the dot of one-thirty. Her long dress rustled as she walked down the path, and when she paused at the door of his car to gather up the folds and slip into the front seat, it was like a movement rehearsed a thousand times. Her mother watched her departure from the door, her father from behind the living-room curtain.

Her mother said: 'Isn't she awfully young?'

'It'll broaden her horizons,' her father replied, 'that's only the front path out there, not the aisle.'

The house that night seemed empty without Lynn. Her parents sat watching the television through to the end of programmes. Gordon came in at about twelve and wondered out loud how Cinderella was getting on.

'You give over,' snapped his mother, 'and leave her alone. And don't torture her tomorrow and upset her with your talk, you hear . . .'

They didn't wait up for her to come in, but for all the sleep she got through worrying about Lynn, her mother might just as well have done. She couldn't understand how her husband in the bed beside her could get to sleep so quick and sound with his only daughter out in the wee small hours and 'broadening her horizons' as he put it.

The luminous green hands of the clock said one-forty. They were late. Time meant nothing to young ones, of course. She'd been like that herself – hating the timetables set for her by other people. You don't understand, when you're young, how parents are obliged to imagine the worst . . .

She couldn't even remember which hotel the dance was at. At two-fifteen she had it in her mind to waken Bill and ask him, when she heard the key in the lock.

She was quickly out of bed and to the head of the stairs. Some giggling reached her, then quiet.

Should she speak down to them or not? It might be as well to let them know she knew they were back.

'Are you there, Lynn?'

A pause, then, 'Yes, Mummy, Michael's just going. I'll be up in a minute or two.'

'Put the chain on the door, dear.'

Back in bed she counted the minutes, and wondered if the next few years were going to be difficult with Lynn. Somehow boys weren't the same. She didn't worry about Gordon so much and, anyway, he hadn't the same spirit in him to go to these places.

Just before three she heard the sound of his car leaving the street, and she was able to content herself with the fact that the dance was over.

When Lynn woke the next morning and swung her feet out of bed, she sat for a moment and wondered how her head was so clear and her body so fresh after the activities of the night before. She'd hardly been off her feet the whole time, except during the meal. Getting through that heap of food had been like a day's work.

It was twelve-thirty by the clock on the bedside table. Lynn skipped down the stairs to the phone.

'Is that you, Lynn?' she heard her mother shout. 'Lunch!'

'In a minute, Mummy, I'm just phoning Gillian if she's in.'

There was no 'if' about it. She knew Gillian would be in and waiting for every pick of news.

'Well, Gillian, I went! Yes. No, listen. I'm in the hall. Five *Babychams*. Well it's a lot for me, Gillian, you know how I giggle and go on. Shh! I'm only in the hall, they'll hear me. If they knew what state Michael was in driving me home I swear they'd kill me, Gillian, they would, stone dead. U-huh. The only thing is, Michael's not bad but I'd rather you-know-who had asked me. I know he's not in the rugby club, but that doesn't stop you *going*, Gillian. But he was nice, though, a big lamb. He went out once, I think to throw up, but he wasn't the only one and one of them stripped down to his underpants – yes! The hairy big thing. Then he got up on the piano and started playing it with his bare feet. Gillian, you should have been there. No, I didn't know anybody – wait, I tell a lie, once I turned a corner and there was this gorgeous-looking creature in front of me in a turquoise evening gown. No, Gillian, it was me in a mirror. Sort of to one side, you know that classical look, my hair seemed to do whatever I told it, you know that sort of way? U-huh. Oh, lovely, veal cutlets. The tableware was out of this world. My people are so working class, Gillian, honest to God, it was like another way of life to be sitting there cutting up all kinds of everything with a hundred different knives and forks. I had to show him which to use first. He hadn't a clue, Gillian, honestly, men know nothing. Next time I'll go with a middle-aged *divorcé* with grey temples. Atmosphere, it's all about atmosphere, Gillian, you should have been there. Yes. U-huh. I hear them shouting at me for breakfast. Well all right, *lunch*. I'll come round later on. Bye.'

Preparations for lunch were well advanced when Lynn made an entrance to the kitchen. Her mother smiled, asked if she'd had a nice time but didn't press for details. Her father remarked lightly that she was going to bed early that night so's she'd be down for bacon and eggs tomorrow morning.

Lynn didn't feel hungry as she sat down at table. A loaf spilled in slices out if its wrapper, and at each of four places the lettuce leaves of a humble salad flounced over the edges of a plate to skirt the surface of a soiled cloth. The old and battered tea-pot, favoured for its easy pour, squatted in its accustomed place at the centre of the table.

It was all so haphazard, so utterly familiar! As she watched her mother trying to do a hundred things at once, Lynn wondered if she would ever be dominated by her own kitchen when she got married.

'How's the boyfriend, then?' Her ridiculous brother started his senseless banter before he even sat down. Lynn knew better than to get angry. So far as Gordon was concerned, the object of the game was to get her angry. He was such a big child for someone in his second year at college.

'Mummy, have you a clean spoon for the sugar? This one's caked hard and lumpy.'

'Fussy, aren't we?' Gordon chipped in.

Lynn ignored him, of course, but in actual fact there was a lot to be fussy about. Because she wasn't hungry herself, Lynn seemed to notice all the more the way her father chewed with his mouth open, the flecks of burned toast in the butter, the filthy thick glar round the cap of the sauce bottle.

'Just a cup of tea for me, please,' Lynn said. 'I'm not that hungry at the moment.'

After lunch Gordon went to play tennis with some unsuspecting girl who couldn't possibly know what he was really like. Lynn told her parents some of the more innocent happenings of her night out, and then, in her serious voice, she said, 'Actually, there is something I'd like to discuss with you.'

There followed a considerable silence, followed by an 'Oh?' from her mother, the non-committal sound of someone who is not sure that she wants to hear more.

'Speak up, love,' said her father, 'there's only your mum and me and the kitchen sink.'

'Well, it's just that I don't like the way we . . . you know, the way we sometimes eat.'

Her mother lifted one or two dishes from the table and carried them to the sink. Her father looked at her hard, and rather grimly.

'Mother, she doesn't like the way we eat.'

'So I hear. Ask her what's wrong with it.'

'What's wrong with what we eat?'

'It's very hard to put into words.'

'Try,' her father said dryly. 'I'm sure you'll manage.'

Lynn chose to address the milk jug as if she was getting answers from it. She had meant to keep this conversation light.

'It's not *what* we eat, it's how. It's got . . . no atmosphere, if you see what I mean.'

'Mother, our eating has no atmosphere in it,' her father echoed; and Lynn, blushing, rushed to her own defence.

'I don't mean we should have endless curries and fancy cheeses and veal cutlets all the time, it's *how* we eat – it's so . . . *plain*.'

With her hands buried in the depths of the tea-towel, Lynn's mother faced her daughter. She stood with her head askance, as if to discover some other meaning in what she had just heard.

'Is there anything else you don't like about us?' she asked.

Lynn shook her head, trying to indicate that this was not what she'd meant.

'Maybe we should change the way we talk, too?' her mother went on regardless.

'No!' Lynn said, alarmed by how big the issue had become in the space of a few sentences. 'Daddy, it's not fair, I didn't mean it like that.'

'It sounds fair to me,' her father said. 'I think you've got a bloody nerve, if you want to know.'

Lynn, by no means a child but still not a woman, looked her in-between self as she fought back tears of resentment at her parents' misunderstanding, which seemed almost deliberate. The responsibility of standing there and defending her position seemed altogether too much for her. Rather than take on both of them at once, she left the room.

The mother looked at the father, whose face showed the dilemma in his mind: whether to feel hurt or feel angry.

'So much for broad horizons,' she said in a matter-of-fact way.

The adversaries in this word-battle did not meet again until tea-time, when the family gathered once more round the kitchen table to eat. Gordon was totally bewildered by what went on. His mother wore her necklace of imitation pearls as she uncorked a bottle of red wine and delivered a slurp into each of four cut-crystal glasses. His father, wearing the overalls he'd been painting in, spread a linen napkin over his knee and said of the wine: 'Delicate nose.' Lip-lip-lip, smack-smack. 'Hmm. Dusty, dark, and slightly nutty.' Lip-lip, smack-smack. 'Delicious. It takes a decent red for steak, what do you think, Lynn?'

Gordon was amazed that his garrulous sister had nothing to say, for there was a talking point no matter where he looked. That candle for a start! He lifted one of the heavy, pearl-handled knives lying by his plate and balanced it on his finger. Every piece of cutlery on the sparkling table matched its fellow.

'Lah-dee-dah,' Gordon said. 'Are we expecting Her Majesty?' He was informed, ever so politely, to mind his own business when he inquired if Father had won the pools at last. Glancing over to Lynn for a sign that he'd come home to the right house, he saw her sitting there with her head down.

Gordon asked, when the meal began: 'Is it this knife here?'

'You start at the outside and work in,' his mother told him, 'as you know rightly.'

'One day, my lad,' said his father, 'you may need to know these things. If you work hard, you too might join the ranks of the aristocrockery. We don't want to be disgraced, do we, Lynn? Lynn?'

'Yes, that's right,' Lynn said with some hostility.

'He was only a fitter's son, they'll say, but he picked up every pea on his fork.'

The rest of Lynn's Saturday night passed rapidly by. First Michael phoned and had to be told that she wasn't able to go out after coming in late the night before. Then she was asked to do the dishes so that her mother could see the detective movie on TV for a change. It took her a full hour, for every dish in the house seemed to have been used in the preparation of the six-course meal, and every knife, fork and spoon had to be thoroughly dried and slotted into a special box with a satin finish inside. Gladly she went to bed early and read.

The last person she saw that day was Gordon, who gave a timid little knock on her door and came in.

'What is going on in this *house*?' he asked, subdued for once.

'Nothing,' said Lynn.

'They were OK when I left them at lunch. Then I arrive back to the Mad Hatter's tea-party. You know what they're at now? They're curled up on the settee like it's lovers' lane. In the dark. They're drinking blood-red wine and watching Dracula.'

'I criticised their eating habits,' Lynn said quietly. 'It's their revenge.'

'When? How?'

'At lunch-time. I only said everything was a bit plain, it didn't have any style.'

Gordon took a moment or two to fit this information into what he already knew of the day's events. Eventually, he got the picture. It quite shocked Lynn to see how seriously he took her confession. Normally everything was a big joke to him.

'So that's it! You mean . . . because of what you said to them they went out and bought all that table stuff? They need their heads examined.'

On his way out, Gordon flicked off her light just to annoy her.

'And where did the old man get the money for it all?' his silhouette said from the door. 'He's always pleading poverty, says he hasn't two pennies to rub together. He'll not have now, that's for sure.'

'Switch on my light,' Lynn snapped at him.

'Switch it on yourself. Snob!'

Lying there in the dark above the morbid music of the late-night horror film, Lynn went twenty-four hours back in time to see herself in turquoise blue, sitting at the long dining table like a nervous little girl being inspected at the Guides. She'd known the knives and forks in theory, but among those confidently talking people, she'd fumbled and waited for Michael's lead. With shame she remembered her impulse to let people know her age so that they could make allowances for her.

Lynn made a silent promise to herself. When she became a woman she would do things in style, and if that made her a snob, too bad.

Meanwhile, in the living-room below her, the level of wine in the second bottle of Australian red had sunk well below the label. An argument was in progress. He swore it had been Great-Aunt Queenie, but she insisted she ought to know, for her own bridesmaid Joanna had bought her the beautiful set of cutlery which, for twenty years, had seemed much too grand to use.

Time wounds all heels.

Anon.

The Sleeping Beauty of Anton P'ntarr

Time will run back, and fetch the age of gold.

John Milton.

The action in this love story happens on a planet far from here called Clemess Amara. When the stars and several moons come out over Clemess Amara, you can see, in the southern sky, a constellation known as Hoth's Crib.

Hoth and his wife had lived in ancient times when people were much the same as nowadays, except that they didn't die. There was no sickness and everybody lived for ever. Poor old Hoth was the one who changed all that. Hoth's wife had a baby-sitting job. She nursed the baby son of Waina, a top goddess of that time, and that's how the trouble started. Other gods and goddesses were always trying to steal this baby, so Waina made a magic crib to keep him safe.

'While my baby sleeps,' she said to Hoth's wife, 'you must always rock him in the cradle so that he is never still. So long as the baby is rocking, no harm can come to him.'

One day Hoth's wife went to market, leaving Hoth in charge of the baby. Silly old Hoth nodded off himself in front of a roaring fire, and when he woke up there was a wizened Changeling in the crib instead of Waina's pink and lovely baby. Poor Hoth tried to make a few excuses, but the gods don't listen much when mortals try to explain themselves.

'Your punishment shall be the creature in the crib,' Waina called out in a voice that seemed to roll down from the hills. 'It shall grow and prosper, and in due time the peoples of this race shall meet with it face-to-face, and individually.' The Changeling grew, and prospered, and pursues us all to this day. Its name is Death.

How Anton P'ntarr loved that girl from the Inner-Space Menagerie! Every time he saw her his heart beat on his ribs as though it wanted let out of its cage.

He watched her feeding a Squit in its tank. The Squit's green head lay flat on the water rather like a pretty lily, and here ended the resemblance to flowers. Squits had teeth sharp enough to take your finger off. Then she checked the pressure in the cage inhabited by the Hairy Gloop from the planet Perseus. This was a heavy-gravity planet and poor Hairy Gloops exploded if the pressure dropped below fifty-five kilos per square centimetre. *Pop!* they went.

Anton P'ntarr wondered, by no means for the first time, what had made this girl choose to work at the Inner-Space Menagerie. The school sent her here for two days a week as part of a work-experience course. She could have taken Lunar Catering or any one of a number of interesting options, but she chose instead to come into this zoo, this huge crystal ball flooded with light, where the trustees had assembled a collection of life-forms from the nearer planets. Ugly things, most of them, but their foul habits and vile perfumes were not enough to keep Anton P'ntarr away. He came here often to observe his beauty among the beasts.

And today was rather a special day, for he had resolved to approach her, speak to her, let her know at last that he existed. He stood beside the transparent den where they kept the Wheebler from the planet Dracena.

Oh, beating heart be still! He spoke his first words to her: 'That's a very fine Wheebler you've got there.'

'Yes, isn't it gorgeous?' she said.

No, Anton P'ntarr did not find it gorgeous. Frankly, the thing was revolting from all angles. The Wheebler resembled a large lump of dough and possessed the power to deliver an electric shock of 1000 volts. It could, besides, mould itself into any shape or form – or even, when in the mood, turn itself inside out.

'They begin life as a vegetable, you know,' she said. 'They're really one of the miracles of the Universe.'

'I can easily believe it,' replied Anton P'ntarr.

He wanted to tell her that she, too, was one of the miracles of the Universe. Her shining hair, piled high on her head in the latest fashion, rose fully half a metre into the air, the various strands of it held in place by a lattice of light wire. Careful girls kept this hidden, of course. Also, round the rims of her ears, she wore coils of dull gold. Anton P'ntarr knew he had been guilty of staring and cleared his throat for the little speech he had prepared.

'Perhaps I should say who I am. My name is Anton P'ntarr and I'm in your Compulsory Ecology classes at school.'

'Oh, they're so boring, aren't they?'

'They are indeed. I'm hoping to be a dentist, myself.'

She pushed some food pills through the tiny holes in the Wheebler's pen and the great lump heaved itself about in excitement.

'A dentist,' she said. 'Isn't that a bit old-fashioned in this day and age?'

The silly girl seemed unaware of the fact that the human race has always relied rather heavily on its teeth. 'Teeth are important,' said Anton P'ntarr, but gently. He didn't want an argument. 'You shouldn't overlook the cultural persistence of the white smile.'

She smiled at him whitely. 'The cultural persistence of the . . . what? The white smile? That doesn't mean anything, it's just nonsense.'

It probably was, but what did it matter when she was talking to him. He walked with her to the area reserved for the Whooping Primates of Cedonia.

'No it's not. We *could* have red, green and orange teeth. The multi-coloured smile is perfectly feasible nowadays, but do people want it? They do not. The white smile is here to stay and so are dentists.'

She looked at him out of two of nature's perfect gems, illuminated from within by her natural radiance. Anton P'ntarr hoped that he would not get carried away and say something stupidly romantic.

'Are you wise or have you a chromosome loose?' she asked him.

'Please tell me your name.'

'Why?'

'So that I can say it to myself, over and over again.'

'You are missing a chromosome,' she said, flicking open a gate labelled Authorised Personnel Only. The Whooping Primates had recognised her by now and had taken to screaming for their bellies to be filled. It was a rather desperate Anton P'ntarr who shouted after her, 'Well then, can I call you on the Visiphone?'

'Excuse me,' she replied. 'I have to feed the Whooping Primates of Cedonia.'

Nuts, nuts and more nuts to the Whooping Primates of Cedonia, thought Anton P'ntarr as he walked home across the roofs of the city; and he suffered with every step from the pangs of unrequited love.

Really, it was pathetic what she had reduced him to. And without knowing it! She didn't understand how powerful she was. He even felt jealous of the revolting Wheebler from the planet Dracena because she thought it was gorgeous . . . Thoughts like these kept him busy until he reached home.

Anton P'ntarr lived with his father, his mother, his two brothers and his little sister, Leena, in one of the fashionable Troglodyte Dwellings on the fringes of Ule.

These Troglodyte Dwellings were actually holes in the chalk hillside – caves. In the distant past they had probably been inhabited by primitive people, advanced cousins of the Whooping Primates of Cedonia; millions of years later they had become a status symbol, and the smartest thing you could say at a party was, 'Just moved, you know, into one of the Troglodyte Dwellings.' Anton P'ntarr's mother had warned her children never, *never* to refer to their home as a cave, especially not in company. His mother was a dedicated snob, but he was fond of her just the same.

When he returned home to his cave that evening, he found the family assembled in one room; and quite clearly, something had excited them.

'Guess what!' Leena yelled after plonking a smacker of a kiss on his nose. 'Guess, Anton, guess oh guess!'

'Can't,' said Anton P'ntarr, who was in no mood for silly games. He noticed his mother's eyes. Shining, they were, in the failing light. 'Well? Isn't anybody going to tell me?'

'Anton. Oh, Anton,' said his mother. 'We finally got six Permits, my dear. We are all going on a time sleep. For a hundred and fifty years. Isn't it wonderful?'

That heart of his which had taken such a pounding this day began to act up again.

'A time sleep!' he managed to splutter.

His father held up six small, metal discs, rarer than gold dust. Their Permits to travel – you couldn't go without one. 'The whole family!' said Father P'ntarr, and little Leena danced about on tiny bare feet, chanting, 'We're going to be frozen, clap hands. We're going to be frozen, clap hands.'

Frozen. The popular, if erroneous, term for human hibernation. All six of them would be put into cold storage and woken up at some future date to savour the flavour of life in another time. You could 'Travel On' for two hundred years, one hundred and fifty years or for ninety-nine years and a day – whichever took your fancy.

'Isn't it exciting?' he heard his mother exclaim. 'Think how different the world will be in the century after next, can you *imagine*?' And they all started talking at once, as if they were discussing some inconsequential thing like a family holiday on the moons of Tyre.

Said Anton P'ntarr: 'I'm not going.'

He certainly was not. He could see no point in breaking off the perfectly successful life he was enjoying in the here and now, in order to take it up again at some notional time in the future. Definitely not. He told them again, 'You can throw my Permit away. I'm not going.'

'Oh, Anton!' said his mother. 'You always were such a stubborn child.'

A row occurred. He got it hot and heavy from all sides. First they threatened him. They said they would get a Compulsory Order and *make* him come with them, but he calmly pointed out that he was too old by a few weeks for a Compulsory Order to be binding on him. Then they wheedled. 'Think of all the sacrifices made for you,' they said, 'and you won't even come into the future with us. Oh, Anton, *why* won't you come into the future with us? It's the perfect way to escape from the ruts and routines of life in the metropolis.'

'I'm not in a rut,' said Anton.

'But you will be,' they said. 'And you'll never get another chance. Each person gets only one Permit, only one. Tens of thousands of people are scheming and bribing to get Permits, they said, it's such an *honour* to be selected, for goodness sake. Only the best people are chosen for Travelling On, no convicts or degenerates are sent forward, none of your rabble. 'The cream of society,' said his mother, as if this were the most irrefutable argument of all. 'Only the very *cream.*'

'I'm staying put,' said Anton P'ntarr.

After a day like that was it any wonder he had a blasted dream?

The revolting Wheebler escaped from its pen and got among the general public. There were horrendous scenes. People were trampled underfoot and others fainted clean away as the thing squeezed itself into a worm three or four kilometres long and surrounded the Ecology Building. But help was at hand. To the astonishment of all who were privileged to be there that day, Anton P'ntarr donned rubber gloves and shoes and rolled it up like a hosepipe and returned the Wheebler to the Inner-Space Menagerie. He was made an honorary member of that great zoo and what's-'er-name nearly hugged his head off for being such a hero.

He woke up in a sweat, quivering with fear at the thought of what he'd just done. He might have had 1000 volts up his arms and been fried to a frazzle! 'If today is like yesterday,' Anton P'ntarr promised himself, 'I shall not get up tomorrow.'

He took a decision. He quickly jumped out of bed and punched her Central Registration Number into the Visiphone before he lost his nerve. And suddenly there she was, glaring out at him from the screen on the wall.

She didn't look pleased. 'It's you. You've no business calling me at this time of the morning. I'm not fit to be seen.'

No doubt about that. The lattice of light wire was still very apparent under her hair. Clearly she had not yet finished her toilette.

'I don't care what you look like,' said Anton P'ntarr. 'You are the object of all my affections.'

'What?'

'I love you.'

'Don't be so silly, you hardly know me.'

'Tell me your name. I sneaked your initials and your number from school but I don't know what to call you.'

'If you must know, it's Elena Mede Shahadnazar. My friends call me Mede.'

Not a bit of wonder, he thought. Elena Mede Sha . . . Shazahad . . . 'Can I call you Mede, too?'

'You can if you like. You don't have to be in a secret society to call me Mede, I'm a very ordinary person.'

Ordinary! She didn't know, she had no idea. 'Not to me. You're a goddess to me.'

'Is that a fact? Which one?'

He couldn't come up with the name of a goddess quickly enough, so he changed the subject. 'Will I see you in school? Are you going to Compulsory Ecology at the end of the week?'

'Yes, worse luck.'

'Meet me on the roof during break. Please. I'll protect you from the Waps and Wazza-wazzas.'

That made her grin a little. She examined her cuticles, keeping him waiting. 'All right, I'll meet you on the roof.'

The screen went blank, but it made no difference – he could still see her sitting there, putting the finishing touches to that impossible hair-do. 'Mede,' he said. Mede, what a lovely name. And Mede and Mede and more Mede.

He had a thought on the way to school that morning. Maybe he should tell his parents about her, then they wouldn't keep at him to go disappearing off into the future. Imagine! He could wake up in the century after next madly in love with somebody who'd already been dead a hundred years. Surely they must see that *they* were the unreasonable ones in this dispute, and not him.

Thoughts such as these slowed him down so that he was late for school. His personal computer waited patiently for him with a message. 'Student to be warned,' it whispered. Anton P'ntarr hit the registration key to show that he was present, and snarled, 'Satisfied?' The face of the teacher appeared on the computer screen, the lights were dimmed and morning lectures commenced. Like the other thousand-odd pupils in the theatre, Anton P'ntarr heard why life died out on boring old planets like Earth and Ithica Three. And he wondered which lucky beast was being fed by Elena Mede Shazna . . . Shanazda . . . whatever – down at the zoo.

That same afternoon the six members of the P'ntarr family travelled by Zoomtube to the centre of the city, where they disembarked and climbed the worn sandstone steps of the oldest building in the city of Ule.

This was the Institute of Longevity. They were on their way to be measured up for their travelling caskets and to receive the first of their anti-dream injections – except for Anton P'ntarr, who accompanied them merely in the role of observer. He still wasn't going.

At the entrance to the Institute, Father P'ntarr made them stop to marvel at one of the magnificent sights of the metropolis – the door. It towered above them at least twenty metres high, and in its entirety constituted the largest wooden artefact to have survived from the ancient civilisations of Clemess Amara. Into the centre of the door, some anonymous craftsmen had carved the mythological Hoth staring into his crib.

Little Leena recognised the look of agony on Hoth's face. 'Oh, look, Mummy, we've got that man in our cave.'

So they had. A cheap ornament of Hoth sat in an alcove near the window. Mother P'ntarr took her daughter firmly by the hand.

'Come along, dear. And don't say "cave". We live in a Troglodyte Dwelling.'

The P'ntarrs walked the length of the Institute's central hall, the roof of which was carried high on slim colonnades of red, unpolished stone. The architects of this place – so it seemed to Anton P'ntarr – had been trying to make human beings feel small. Every little sound they made returned to them with interest, like a reproach. Mother P'ntarr was busy saying, 'Shh!' to nobody in particular, when suddenly an official-looking gentleman stepped out from behind a pillar and startled them all.

'The P'ntarr family, I presume?'

'Correct, sir,' said Father P'ntarr, never one to lose his composure for long. 'We are here in our entirety.'

'Hmm. This way, please. We like to do our measuring in the Time Terminal.'

He had a mincing sort of voice, this official gentleman, and a tendency to rub his hands together under his chin. He led them through to a place where a sign said:

TIME TERMINAL:

THIS ESTABLISHMENT IS DEDICATED

TO THE CONQUEST OF MANKIND'S

MOST DEDICATED PURSUER, THE

CHANGELING DEATH.

Several caskets were prominently displayed on a slowly-revolving stand. These caskets, about two metres long, appeared to be made of metal. Father P'ntarr did as the official gentleman said and climbed rather bashfully into one of the turning caskets to try it out. It had purple lining. Watching his father travelling slowly round in circles, Anton P'ntarr thought he had never in his life seen anything so daft.

'All you need is a pair of oars, Dad. You could row into the future.'

'Anton!' said his mother.

She felt the purple lining between finger and thumb.

'It also comes in pink or blue, Madam. The casket itself is our very best alloy. Note the brass handles for easy lifting – ornamental but useful, like all the best art. You'll just love this casket, Sir.'

Father P'ntarr waited until the revolving stand brought him back to his family. Raising his head from a horizontal position, he said, 'I must say it feels rather comfortable.'

'That lining, Madam. Real silk.'

'Really?'

'Oh yes! Real natural fibre. You'll just love waking up in this, Madam.'

'How do you know?' grunted Anton P'ntarr. 'You'll not be there to see her get up.'

'Anton!' his mother rebuked him. 'That's enough. Just because you've decided not to go, there's no need to mock.' By way of explanation she added to the official, 'He says he's in love.'

'Huh!' said the official, as if all was now clear. He took a computer from his pocket and recorded details about each member of the travelling party so that people would know a little about them when the time came to thaw them out in the century after next. Finally, he coughed and addressed Mother P'ntarr on a delicate matter.

'Does Madam have a choice of travelling garment?'

'Oh . . . I thought . . . I have a very pretty blue nightdress.'

'Very tasteful. Most appropriate.'

'It would go with the blue lining.'

'It absolutely would. May I quietly recommend a little rouge for the long sleep? After one or two hundred years one is apt to wake up a little . . . you know . . . a little wan.'

But would she come, he wondered?

All the week he had that question at the back of his mind: would his Elena Mede keep that promise to meet him on the roof of the Ecology Building? After a morning's study of fossils of cycads and ferns and petrified ammonites he escaped at last to the heights of the city and saw her waiting for him among the exotic blooms. The roofs of Ule were famous for their flowers. Seeds, gathered by interstellar spacecraft from the planets of the Semule Plain, had been planted all over the place with incredible profusion, so that every insect now thought of this fragrant corner of the world as Paradise. Waps and Wazza-wazzas buzzed around the head of Elena Mede Shaznawhatever – the fairest flower of all. A wind had got up, and because of her kite-like hairstyle, which was an affront to common sense, she came towards him listing.

'Well,' she said, 'fancy keeping a goddess waiting.'

He felt really quite shy. As they began to walk it occurred to him that there was one brute of a problem about being so mightily under some other person's spell: you felt so *unworthy* when you were with her. Fortunately an enormous Wap began to orbit her head. Anton P'ntarr reached over and annihilated the insect with a satisfying *splat*!

'How are the animals?' he asked.

'Oh, fine.'

'What do the Whooping Primates think of your hair piled up like that? Hair in the air, so to speak.'

'I didn't ask them.'

'Best not to.'

She flung a critical glance in his direction. 'I didn't come up here to be insulted, so be careful.'

'I'm not insulting you. I've been saying your name all morning. Mede and Mede and Mede. Please – come Layering with me.'

Layering: the perfect sport for lovers since it provided plenty of opportunities for physical contact if people wanted it – and, of course, most people did. While Mede considered her answer, Anton P'ntarr looked away across the roofs of the city to where the sun picked out the spindly minarets of the Institute of Longevity. Not much to cheer him up in that direction. A few weeks more and his parents would be stretched out stiffer than a couple of icicles.

Said Elena Mede Shahadnazar: 'All right. I'll come.'

Perhaps a majority of the wooers of maidens are deeply pessimistic at the beginning of a romance. Certainly Anton P'ntarr could hardly believe his ears.

'You will?'

'Yes, it might be fun.'

'You'll come Layering with me?' He executed a hugely buzzing Wazza-wazza in celebration. 'Oh, Mede, my one and only cherished one.' And he seized her hand, and began to gobble it.

She said, 'Come on, stop that when people are looking. I'll come Layering with you, but I don't want any funny business when we get into the Bubble. Is that fair enough, Anton?'

'Oh absolutely,' said Anton, with the air of one who despises funny business.

'And stop slaughtering insects. Even Wazza-wazzas have a role to play in the ecological pyramid of life.'

Their relationship prospered. Even his mother stopped saying things like, 'Really, Anton, if you would just give yourself a good shake and get her out of your system', and accepted the fact that her eldest son had found a most powerful motive for remaining in the present time.

Besides, he was quite right. He was just three months too old for them to get a Compulsory Order.

Oh but there were tears, of course, and tantrums as the day approached when the family would be split for ever. Anton went with them to the Institute of Longevity and, to please his mother, accompanied them into the Time Terminal for a session of last goodbyes.

His father took his hand firmly, and whispered quietly that one could be certain of nothing in this life.

'Listen, son, I really must say this to you. Affairs of the heart are notoriously fickle.'

'I know that, Dad.'

'You're embarrassed, of course,' said his dad, turning red, 'but if you *do* want to come after us . . .'

Anton P'ntarr shook his head. Not again! 'I won't.'

'Fair enough. Just remember to look in Hoth's Crib.'

'Good luck in the future, Dad,' said Anton P'ntarr.

His mother wailed that she would never see her grandchildren. 'Take pictures of them, won't you? We'd like to see them before they die.'

Yes, yes, of course he would leave film for them to see. And he kissed them one by one.

'I'll be famous by the time you lot wake up,' he said cheerfully, adding to Leena, 'You'll be learning about me in your history classes. That'll be a laugh.'

He stayed until they received the last of their anti-dream injections, then left them to get on with their long sleep.

The swamps at Doonacre.

A deadly wasteland. From this area beyond the boundaries of the city, hissing clouds of crimson, white and pale grey gases rose hundreds of metres into the air. Nothing ventured through Doonacre, neither on foot nor on the wing. And yet, from a long way off Doonacre you could see large, transparent bubbles rising and falling at different speeds through the colourful miasma. To the untrained eye they looked like uncommonly fragile and beautiful natural phenomena: in fact these were man-made Bubbles, and they had people in them, for this was the latest entertainment craze for the citizens of Ule. One moment you went rolling down the dips caused by different densities of gas; the next you were flattened against the curved wall of your Bubble, on your way with a whoosh! to yet another pinnacle of pressure. On their rest days, Anton and Mede went Layering, as a rule.

They found it exciting to tempt fate by tumbling through layers of noxious gas in a Bubble of oxygen – and it was private, too, way up there in the shifting, vivid sky: the perfect place, in fact, for young people who wanted a bit of slap and tickle with their rough and tumble. On one of their Layering days – it was to be their last – Anton P'ntarr said to his Elena Mede, 'My mother wants to see photos of my children. I bet you and I could make little beauties.'

She didn't answer, so he continued merrily, 'I could look after their teeth and you could tell them stories about the bunch of horrors down at the zoo. Any new beasties?'

She sat staring out through the wall of the Bubble at another couple drifting upwards. They were locked in a clinch and clearly using up their oxygen at a fearful rate.

'Disgraceful,' said Anton P'ntarr.

'Yes,' said Mede, 'we received a Malasander Bird from Colon Four. They live inside the rims of volcanoes.'

'Beats a Troglodyte Dwelling any day.'

'The Malasander male vomits up its food to impress its mate, it's a fascinating courtship display. Glands in the throat turn the contents of the stomach bright green.'

Oh yuk. Hoth's Teeth, thought Anton. Not to be outdone by the Malasander male from Colon Four, he told her his dream, the one about the escaped Wheebler, and explained how he had risked 1000 volts to save everybody's life, and all for the love of Elena Mede Sha . . . Shaznadahar . . . ?

'Well, I know,' he finished modestly, 'that it doesn't compare with bright green *vomit*, but you've got to admit it was pretty good.'

'Oh,' she suddenly declared with a rush of words, 'I do love you, Anton P'ntarr.'

But she was sitting there with tears in her eyes. He straightened her up with a hand on either shoulder. 'Mede. What's wrong with you today?'

'I'm sorry,' she said, composing herself. 'I've really been quite brave about it until now. Mind you, they only told me yesterday.' And she sniffed before adding bitterly, 'We've been selected.'

'What for?'

'Anton! You can *guess* what for.'

He stood up in the Bubble until his head hit the rubbery circumference. Of course he could guess. It was happening to him again.

'But you can refuse to go!' he shouted.

'Can't. I can't, Anton. They've taken out a Compulsory Order for me. I have to go.'

Their Bubble was sinking with a soft hiss through a scarlet cloud with a foaming black heart. What brutal people parents could be, he was thinking, when they really put their minds to it. He asked her an academic question. 'How long?'

'On, Anton. Ninety-nine years and a day.'

Away she went from him. 'Travelling On' without moving a muscle, leaving him a prisoner in the present time, and pining for her as if he were one of the uglies down at the Inner-Space Menagerie.

Anton P'ntarr had grown up in a city to which there were two tiers. Over the centuries, the roof of Ule had gradually evolved into a vast precinct for the exclusive use of pedestrians. Hundreds of narrow bridges – from the ground they seemed marvellously delicate things, like the work of spinning insects – linked each roof to the next in an ongoing promenade of gardens, observatories, blue lakes and numerous other amenities. There were seven hundred such bridges in Ule. During the days following the departure of his Elena Mede, Anton P'ntarr walked every one of them. He had the air of one whose spirit has taken leave of the body, and flown.

Ninety-nine years and a day. Well, they might as well let her sleep for one day short of never, for all it mattered now.

Oh yes, he conceded mordantly, he might see her again. People could expect to cheat the Changeling for a hundred and twenty years and more if they looked after themselves. He'd be a hundred and fifteen years old when she woke up. He could see himself an old man with a beard down to his toes, standing in an unobtrusive place in the Time Terminal, watching her emerge, so fresh, so young, still beautiful, his unattainable, unapproachable, lovely Mede.

Would she look round? Would she remember and look round for him, just in case? Oh! To have his Permit, to sleep that long sleep and be wakened the day before her, then to raise her from the vulgar purple lining with a kiss! Ye gods, ye gods, he was thinking, what cruel blows Humankind is made to bear.

He caught sight of old Hoth up there in the southern sky, bent over his Crib, a face on him as if he was the daddy of all misery. *He* knew. Poor old Hoth, poor old Anton P'ntarr, two of a kind.

Hoth's Crib . . . ?

He began to walk quickly, feet keeping pace with his mind. There was something his father had said about Hoth's Crib . . .

But what? It had all been rather emotional and embarrassing during their last chats together, all temper and no sense. He hadn't taken any of it in. Until now.

Oh, ye gods – until now! Suddenly his feet wouldn't be content with walking. Mere walking wouldn't do. His feet began to run, his lungs began to ache, his mind soared.

In the Troglodyte Dwelling, he paused, breathless, staring up at the cheap representation of Hoth and warning himself that perhaps, after all, he was mistaken. Surely his father had surrendered the Permit or thrown it away? Anton P'ntarr had told him often enough where he could stick it.

With reverent hands he lifted down the ornament – here was an object which had presided over his childhood and given him dreams. He looked into the Crib. In the hood which traditionally hid the

Changeling's face from human eyes, he saw a bright little disc.

His ticket to ride for ninety-nine years and a day.

And pluck till time and times are done
the silver apples of the moon,
the golden apples of the sun.

W B Yeats.

Miss Hetherington and Me

Stands the church clock at ten to three?
And is there honey still for tea?

Rupert Brooke.

Miss Hetherington was my Sunday School teacher, and for her I wanted to be good.

I wanted to be good, but this was never easy for me. Things beyond my control forced me to be not-so-good, and there were times when I was so bad that I knew Miss Hetherington wouldn't look at me twice if she heard what I'd been up to. Needless to say, I blamed most of my troubles on other people, such as Trevor Moorhead.

One day Trevor Moorhead appeared in our street wearing a six-gun at his hip. He looked impressively quick on the draw, and he could twirl the gun a bit, too, before sticking it back in its tie-down holster. The thing fired caps. Moorhead drew our attention to the actual smoke coming out of the barrel.

'See the smoke? It's the gunpowder does that. Sniff and you'll smell it.'

I wouldn't please him to smell it, and neither would my friend Marcus, for we were half mad with jealousy. Moorhead was in the same class as us and we knew that he always ruled his homework in red ink from a fountain pen with a gold nib. And his father had a Norton like a giant wasp in the backyard. I had sat upon it once. There was plenty about Moorhead to make us jealous without sniffing his gunpowder as well.

'Would you dare to draw against me?' Moorhead asked us slyly.

'I would draw against you,' I said.

'So would I,' said my friend Marcus. 'You wait here till we get our guns.'

Neither Marcus nor I had a six-gun between us, so we nipped into Paxton's field and tore up a big carrot each. Armed with these in our trouser belts, we faced up to Moorhead in our back entry. The signal to go for your gun was a blatter on a bin-lid.

He slaughtered us.

What happened was, you made a desperate lunge for your carrot, and the thing either slipped down the leg of your trousers or else flew out of your hand, leaving Moorhead all the time in the world to pump you full o' lead.

'You had a real gun, Moorhead!' Marcus pointed out to him.

'Oh aye, blame it on the carrots,' smiled Moorhead. Away he went, slapping leather every third step or so, thinking himself the slickest thing on two legs.

Me and Marcus now had one ambition in life: to outdraw Moorhead and drill him full of daylight.

That night when my father came home, I asked him if he would buy me a six-gun in a holster if I agreed to share it with my brother Harry without fighting over it.

'Do you think I'm made of money?' he said. 'You got new pyjamas last week.'

Pyjamas! I felt a surge of hatred for my new pyjamas. They'd done me out of something I really needed.

'Ah go on, Daddy. Trevor Moorhead has one.'

'And when he gets the measles I suppose you'll want them too.'

After tea, as soon as I saw the kitchen empty, I got up on a stool and cut two cubes off the Sunday jelly, and ate them both. This was to pay them back for buying me pyjamas instead of a six-gun.

The next day Marcus appeared in our backs with a banana sticking out of his pocket. Now a banana wasn't a sight you saw every day back in the summer of 1952. Harry and I counted ourselves lucky if we got our hands on a big watery apple from the country. The banana, it seems, was connected with the Catholic church, for somehow a lorry-load of fresh fruit had come into the possession of the parish priest, and Marcus's mother had bought some cheap in the chapel hall.

That banana sticking out of Marcus's pocket looked just right for grabbing hold of. Marcus glanced at me, then down at his side, and a gleam lit up his eye. He made one smooth lovely motion, and I was staring down the barrel of a banana.

'What do you think?' he said.

'Beautiful,' I said with emotion.

It was my go. Marcus said it was like watching lightning strike. We both knew that Moorhead was dead meat.

Unfortunately, the banana turned to mush on us and we had to eat it. After a sprint down the Longstone we got to the chapel, hoping to arrive in the nick of time to get the last of the bananas; but at the chapel gates, I stopped.

'What's wrong?' said Marcus.

'Nothing. You go.'

'You're afraid,' said Marcus.

'I am not, but they wouldn't give me a banana because I'm a Protestant. You'd better hurry up.'

My mother had told me about Catholics. They were the same as us only different, she said, which satisfied me up to a point. I could see that Marcus was the same as me from Monday to Saturday, but on Sunday he never wore his good clothes all day, while I had to wear mine to bedtime. Another thing I had observed about Catholics was that they were well able to stand the sight of blood. There was – and still is – a Jesus with thorns on his head nailed to a cross outside the chapel and I could never do more than take a scally-eyed glance at it, even while passing in the bus. It never bothered Marcus.

He came back with no bananas. 'They're all away. We'll try down the town.'

'Why, have you money?'

'I think I might have a ha'penny.'

That'll not look near a banana, I thought.

We went down the town anyway, and saw exactly what we were looking for on a stall outside a greengrocer's shop. Two lovely bunches.

'One of us goes into the shop and talks to the man,' said Marcus, 'the other swipes a bunch from the stall. Which do you want to do?'

This was one of those moments when I thought of Miss Hetherington, who was at least sixteen. She wore a white dress with flouncy bits all the way down the front so that she reminded me of a runny ice-cream. Once I held her hat pins while she talked us through the catechism, and I knew she would be sad if I stole bananas. But then I thought of Moorhead.

'I'll do the talking, you swipe them,' I said.

So in I went and asked the man if he could spare me an old cabbage for my rabbit – a mouldy one would do.

'I didn't know they ate cabbages,' he said.

'It's not that well,' I said.

He lifted the nearest cabbage he could reach. 'There you are. That should perk him up.'

There was not a thing wrong with the cabbage that man gave me. It was a great cabbage. His largeness of heart made me want to cry as I raced up the Longstone after Marcus, who was halfway home with the bananas by now.

'And my rabbit isn't sick!' I said out loud. 'I haven't even got one.' Then I dumped the cabbage in somebody's bin, which I also knew to be wrong. Methodists did not waste good food, they sent it away in parcels to poor people in far countries.

Our front garden was a mere hanky of a thing, but it did boast a thick privet hedge to mark the boundary between our house and the street. We shoved the bananas deep into the middle of it until we would need them.

'See you after tea,' Marcus said. 'I'm away to fix up the fight with Moorhead.'

When I walked in the house there was the jelly sitting on the sideboard. I took one look at it and knew I was doomed.

'Well?' my mother said.

'Mummy, I didn't want pyjamas,' I said, panicking.

'You stole that jelly!'

'Only a wee bit,' I blurted out. 'I could have taken the whole packet away and you wouldn't have noticed.'

'Would I not? You cheeky young glipe! Am I supposed to say you're a good boy because you only stole a *bit* of the jelly? Well there will be none of this for you, my lad, not the scrapings of a bowl. And what is Miss Hetherington going to say when she hears about this?'

My mother knew something of my strong feelings for Miss

Hetherington because I talked about her a lot and because Sunday was the only day of the week when I combed my own hair. Miss Hetherington's perfume used to make my mouth water – you could taste it as well as smell it, which gave me the idea that women were attractive to men because they were a superior form of confectionery. Every time I went to the pictures I noticed that it was always the men who kissed the women first, and this confirmed my theory that they tasted nice.

'You'd better not tell her, you'd better not!' I howled, hurling myself on to the settee, where I beat the living daylights out of a fawn cushion. At the same time I pictured the bunch of bananas lurking in the darkness of the hedge, and sobered up a bit.

'Well all right,' said my mother, 'if you've learned your lesson. Tell me you're sorry and you'll not do it again.'

'I'm sorry and I'll not do it again.'

When Marcus called, we paid a careful visit to the front hedge and went off to face Moorhead in a blind corner of Paxton's field. We now had a six-gun for each pocket. As soon as Moorhead stepped into view with his holster tied down I could see the tension in his face – he wasn't up against carrots this time.

He and Marcus faced one another, hands poised, both as grim as death.

'Go!' I yelled as I blattered the bin-lid, and they drew.

There is no doubt that Moorhead was quick; but Marcus was the one who went into a war-dance.

'I beat you!'

'You never did.'

'I got you in the heart, Moorhead. You're dead meat!'

When my turn came I got him in the head, but he refused to die and walked away in a huff.

'You're not getting any of our bananas, Moorhead,' Marcus called after him.

'I don't want them!' he yelled back. 'And you're two cheaters. Anyway, a banana's got no trigger.'

We ate two and a half bananas each.

My father worked overtime that Thursday night. He came home with the rolled-up *Telegraph* in his gaberdine pocket as usual, but he also had a lumpy brown parcel under his arm. What this was I thought I knew, but he made no mention of the parcel until he'd had his dinner and heard *Ray's a Laugh* on the wireless.

'There you are,' says he. 'Open that up and see if it suits.'

Oh lucky day! It was the full works – silver gun, pearly handles, leather holster with tie-down thongs, and ten rolls of caps. I gave him a hug that would have snapped the neck of a lesser man.

'You've to share it between the two of you, mind. It's half Harry's.'

'It's half mine,' said Harry.

But that, I knew, was only a detail. Soon it would be all mine. I had a drawerful of stuff up the stairs that I could swop him for his half share in the six-gun.

'And where do you think you're going?' my mother asked me.

'To see Marcus.'

'Get away up to your bed, which is where Marcus is, I'm sure.

And don't be shooting those caps until the morning comes.'

Harry and I slept in the same bed. That night I stuck the six-gun under my pillow, and he slept with the holster under his. I was too excited to fall asleep at once, so I lay in the dark listening to the water in the pipes and the howls of the neighbourhood dogs. After a while I began to wonder about something: what had I done to deserve this lovely gift out of the blue?

I began to wonder, and I didn't like the answer. I had stolen one of Paxton's carrots, told a lie about a sick rabbit, eaten a quarter of the family jelly, wasted a whole cabbage and pinched five bananas. There was something wrong here. All the Methodists I knew, including my mother, my father, and especially Miss Hetherington, spoke with one voice about such matters: you got punished when you did bad things in this life. So why had I been rewarded with a brand new six-gun?

The answer was clear to me. There had been some sort of mistake. I decided to say nothing.

Some days went by. I think Marcus knew I was worried about the bananas because I didn't have the old enthusiasm for plugging Moorhead full of holes.

'It's all right about the bananas,' he said. 'I told Father Avery about them. He said it was bad, true enough, but there's worse things.'

'You what?'

'I told Father Avery.'

'You *told* somebody?' I howled.

'He's a priest,' Marcus explained. 'He knows about these things.'

But I was in no state to hear more. He's told the priest, I thought, he's gone and told the priest. With chilling logic I saw how the mistake would be put right. A man I'd never seen before would be at my house any minute, a tall Catholic stranger from God, dressed in black. A quarter of a jelly and now five bananas. Oh God, it was the stiff collar for me, no doubt. I'd be skinned alive that night and Harry would be given the gun and the holster to have and to hold for the rest of his life.

'Look, he'll not tell, he'll not tell,' Marcus said. 'It's confession. He doesn't tell anybody your business.' And he added carefully, 'Except maybe Our Lord.'

Our Lord was not my problem. 'What about the greengrocer?' I screeched.

And Miss Hetherington! Could a priest know a Methodist?

'Look,' said Marcus, 'it's OK so long as you're sorry for what you did and don't do it again. Are you sorry?'

'I am sorry.'

'That's all right then. Me and Father Avery talked it over. He said it wasn't a sin to shoot Moorhead so long as we're friends afterwards. He told me he once robbed an orchard, you know.'

'Who?'

'Father Avery.'

On hearing that I could only stare. Would Miss Hetherington rob an orchard? I asked myself. It couldn't happen. Maybe the difference between us and Catholics was bigger than my mother thought.

For the next two days I knew that every knock on our door was the priest coming to shop me. By Saturday night I was more content for, although he might still be dangerous, I knew the next day was Sunday, and that, surely, was his busy day.

In Sunday School a wild thought took me over. Marcus had told the priest; what would happen if I told Miss Hetherington? It would call for a terrible bravery, I saw that clearly, more than you needed for injections, even. I watched her tasty lips move as she read out words with expression.

Could I bear it, could I suffer the disappointment in those eyes that now saw only the goodness in me? No, I couldn't. I realised with a shock that I didn't trust her, not even if she'd robbed two orchards.

Those bananas had come between Miss Hetherington and me. It was a miserable little tick who came up our street that day in his Sunday longs, kicking an empty Woodbine packet. Probably I'd been to Sunday School for the last time. I wanted to turn against her because I couldn't be the way she wanted me to be.

Around seven o'clock the following evening we were all playing in the street when the ice-cream man hooted his horn and threw us into a panic. Once that horn went, you had about a minute and a half to coax a thruppny bit out of your mother's purse; then he drove away to sell his melting tub of ice-cream to the foreigners in the next street.

Marcus had my six-gun on. He flung it over to me in a frenzy. I put it somewhere else and hared in to beg. On those warm evenings when you were thirsty from playing, any one of us would have sold his soul for the price of a poke. And when it was all over and the ice-creams were eaten, I couldn't find the six-gun.

Nobody had seen it. You must have seen it, I said. I swore I'd left it lying on the pavement. Then I launched into such a fit of wailing that I drove them all home.

My mother came out and fetched me, saying, 'Will you give over that crying? I thought you were hurt! Imagine gettin' on like that over an old toy gun.'

My father said he was not indeed buying me another one, I should have looked after the one I had. And Harry said I wasn't getting back the metal soldiers I'd paid him for his share of the six-gun. My bereavement was complete and I was full of self-pity for a week.

The winter went by. In the turn of the year my father took the shears to the privet hedge and came across the six-gun. It was still in its holster, although the fancy leather had become a vile slime. The six-gun itself had rusted through so badly that you couldn't squeeze the trigger or break it open to put the caps in. A Paxton carrot had more style than that dud.

All was clear to me now. On that night when the ice-cream man came, I had shoved the six-gun into the very hedge where we had hidden the stolen bananas, and it had perished there. Something up there in the sky had sorted out that earlier mistake. *This* was how things were meant to be. My mother, my father, and above all Miss Hetherington, were dead right.

That time may cease and midnight never come.

Christopher Marlowe.

Sheffield

Ah! When will this long weary day have end,
And lend me leave to come unto my love?

Edmund Spenser.

Hazel was with Tina when they heard the jeep coming up the road.

'Look at the speed of that thing,' Tina said, 'and there's supposed to be a speed limit.'

A second jeep passed them with a whoosh of air. Hazel saw two young soldiers looking back down the road and she waved. She liked the young ones. Some had a real cheeky way with them.

One of the soldiers sat with a rifle resting along his thigh and, for a second, Hazel found herself in its line of fire.

'Do you think they sit with their fingers on the triggers?' she asked Tina, who was waving madly at the disappearing jeep.

'Stuck-up!' Tina yelled. 'They wouldn't even wave back. They should send us them Scotch ones. They used to wave at you all the time.'

Hazel hated the guns. Her brother Colin knew the name of every weapon used by the British Army but she could never get it out of her head that they fired real bullets. Sometimes the soldiers levelled their guns at the kids coming home from school, and she was sure the army wasn't allowed to do that sort of thing.

The kids in the area knew a lot about the army that didn't get into the papers, like the way they gave the two-fingers sign and the way they called people Irish Paddies or Orange Bs.

All the same, Hazel knew the army had a lot to stick.

When she got home there was a note propped against the kettle. *Away over to Sylvia's to get my hair done. Go to the shops, love and get cooked ham for Daddy's lunch tomorrow.*

Upstairs she changed out of her school uniform. From the window she could see to the end of the street, to the high sheets of corrugated tin round the local army base. Her mother said there used to be a view of open country right out to Divis mountain at the end of the street, but Hazel didn't remember. She could hardly remember when the Troubles started. Now she was seventeen.

Hazel collected Tina on the way to the shops where they bought the cooked ham in something of a hurry. Tina had spotted an army patrol coming down the road, two soldiers on one side, two on the other. The soldier nearest to them seemed nervous. He walked backwards, occasionally tramping in the border of a garden and looking from side to side like something hunted. He was young, not much older than themselves.

'Hey, you, you're lovely. What's your name?'

Tina's voice came as a complete surprise to Hazel. The soldier looked at both of them warily. He seemed to decide that Hazel had spoken, for he said to her: 'Hogey Carmichael.'

'Ooo listen to my accent,' Tina said in a lah-dee-dah tone. 'Where do you come from, Coronation Street?'

The soldier smiled, but kept looking round him. He had one of those rifles that could kill you at a mile, or so Colin said.

'I'm from Sheffield,' he said.

'Have they got a football team?' asked Tina.

'More or less.'

Hazel said quietly, 'They make stainless steel cutlery in Sheffield.'

The soldier and Tina stared at her when she volunteered this piece of information.

'Would you like a piece of cooked ham? Go on, Hazel, show it to him. It's fresh out of the shop.'

Hazel opened the parcel. For some reason the sight of the pink meat exposed to the air made her giggle. The young soldier laughed, too. She liked him.

'No thanks,' he said, 'some other time. I have to go.'

Down the street a corporal or something was waving and Tina was saying, 'Jill Morrison goes with a soldier. You know what she told us at dinner-time? She says if you went out with a soldier you wouldn't look twice at a Belfast fella.'

'Why not?'

'She says they're a real laugh, but if I was a Belfast fella I wouldn't look twice at Jill Morrison. What are you and Alan doing the night?'

Hazel wasn't sure. If her folks were going out she would probably have the house to herself when Alan called. Good. She had a thing or two to say to him.

'I think we'll stay in,' she told Tina.

'I'll be serving behind the bar at the club. If I see you I'll slip you a free one. Watch yourself. Better still, watch Alan.'

After a quick tea of fish and chips, Hazel's parents got ready for a night out with some of their cronies in Glengormley. Her mother complained about Colin, who hadn't come in for his tea.

Before she left, Mum said they would be in no later than twelve. Hazel knew she could depend on that. Her mother was very fussy about coming in for a set time on account of the Troubles. That was why Colin worried her so much.

Alan arrived, and came into the living-room a little apprehensively.

'Sit down if you like,' Hazel told him. 'There's nobody here.'

'Oh. They're out then.'

Confidently he settled himself on the settee as if he expected her to come and snuggle up beside him. Instead she stood looking at him. Appraising him. He was even more handsome now than two years ago when she'd fallen for him in fourth year.

'I smell fish and chips,' he said.

Hazel sat on the settee, leaving a gap between them. 'It's the vinegar you smell,' she replied.

'What's the difference?'

'You might as well get it right as get it wrong. You smell the vinegar, not the fish and chips.'

'OK, *vinegar*. Is something the matter? What's the problem?' He reached out a hand.

'Stay there!' Hazel snapped. 'I don't want you near me.'

'What's up with you? Why do you come out with me if you don't want me near you?'

'I'm not out with you, you're sitting in my house, remember?' Calmly, she put it to him. 'I believe you asked Hilary Tynan if she'd go with you to the disco tomorrow night?'

Alan sighed. 'So that's it.'

'Well did you?'

'I only asked her.'

'And what if she'd said yes? "Tough luck, Hilary, you'll have to go by yourself because I'm taking Hazel." Or was it me for the push? You're a laugh.'

'It was only a bit of banter,' he said. 'I wasn't serious, you know that. I'll nip out for a six-pack and we'll talk it over.'

'Get your six-pack, but you needn't bring it back here. We're through.'

It sank in, then, that she meant what she said. He got up and went out, saying, 'You're wired to the moon. I'll warn the lads about you.' Whatever that meant.

Before her parents came in Hazel went to bed to get away from their bustle and noise. Colin came home first. She heard him come up the stairs to the landing, then up the ladder into the roof-space where he'd made a den for himself.

Sheffield, the soldier, came into her head. Sheffield in his full regalia with the smart wee beret on his head. Tina was right, he *had* been lovely.

And he was different. The rifle made him different. Funny, to hear words from Sheffield in Belfast. Adding up the differences that set him apart from the other boys she knew, Hazel found him quite exciting to think about.

It was quiet tonight. At the weekend there was usually somebody making trouble for somebody, but the worst had been that night of the shooting. The army hit a man with a live bullet and she could see him through the slats of her Venetian blind, lying on the pavement, dying in his very life's blood.

She turned over, sickened, wishing she could stop thinking of such things.

Hazel rose early on Saturday to the sound of her father's voice yodelling in her ears. It was an awful sound, like a voice with gears.

'Daddy, they'll hear you,' she warned him through the bathroom door – they lived at the end of a terrace.

'The lucky people!' her father said.

He didn't much care what other people thought of him. One night at the club he stood up and came out with this song called *China Doll*. Hazel had never heard worse, not even at the club. Her father thought he'd been great.

Downstairs everybody mucked in. Her father turned eggs in the pan as he boasted that he broke fewer yolks than her mother, who winked at Hazel as she wet the tea. Even Colin played a part by bringing in the milk from the door. It was an ordinary Saturday morning – until Tina came round with some news.

'You know thon soldier from Sheffield who wouldn't eat the cooked ham? He's on guard up at the base. Come on for a laugh.'

Hazel came readily, for the prospect of seeing Sheffield again rather pleased her. First, though, she smartened herself up a bit.

At the army base a group of army electricians were fixing up floodlights. Sheffield's job, apparently, was to guard the men up the high poles. Tina walked straight up to him.

'It's us, remember? Cooked ham.'

'Oh, yes, I remember.'

'I've got a packet of biscuits for you.'

Tina produced a packet of Rich Tea from a bag. Hazel thought it was a bit sly of her.

Before accepting the biscuits Sheffield walked over to a soldier with stripes on his arm and had a brief word with him. He came back smiling. 'It's all right this. I'll keep them for later and share 'em with my mates if that's OK.'

'Do you like it over here?' Hazel asked him.

'It's my first tour. It'll be OK if people keep bringing me biscuits.'

Tina pointed to his rifle. 'You ever shoot anybody with that?'

'One or two times.'

'Rubber bullets or real?'

'Both.'

'You ever hit anybody?'

Sheffield shook his head.

'You're a bad shot then,' snorted Tina.

Sheffield the soldier seemed to like Tina's bantering talk. Hazel wasn't very good at it. All of a sudden he turned to Hazel and said, point-blank: 'You remind me of somebody.'

'Somebody nice, I hope.'

'Oh yes,' Sheffield said definitely, 'somebody nice. What's your name?'

'Hazel.'

'Mine's Tina,' said Tina.

Again, Sheffield glanced briefly at his patrol leader. 'I have to go. I appreciate the biscuits.' Then he added, 'There's an army film-show on Monday night in the hall. Do you ever go?' He was looking at Hazel as he spoke, right into her face.

'Sometimes,' she said, looking away.

'Well, then . . . Maybe I'll see you.'

Tina came away pretending to be in a bad mood. 'Huh!' She mimicked the soldier's accent. '"You remind me of somebody nice." He must mean his mother. *You* can bring him biscuits, then!' And she linked Hazel's arm to cross the road.

That Saturday night Hazel helped behind the bar at the club until eleven o'clock. On the way home she saw a crowd gathered under the glare of the lights from the army base. Even before the ambulance arrived Hazel knew that something serious had happened.

Tina was there, near the front of the crowd. Hazel tried to reach out and touch her, but somebody jostled her off balance. Already there were more people pressing from behind, trying to see.

'Tina, what happened? What's wrong?'

The man in front of her turned round. He was Alan's uncle. 'They knocked him down,' he said angrily, 'that's what's wrong. Wouldn't you know?'

Tina gave up her place at the front and joined Hazel. She looked thoroughly shaken, even allowing for the whiteness of her face in the floodlights.

'It's Mr Ringland, he's just lying there with a blanket right over his head. Hazel, they only do that when they're dead, don't they?'

From all sides now came the pressure of bodies, binding them in. Someone shouted, 'That's the bloody army for you! They drive the roads like they own them.'

A murmur rose in agreement as the ambulance began to move, and one voice rose above the others, 'What the hell's your hurry? Sure, isn't the man dead?'

Somebody at the back found that funny, but the main mood was anger. Haze could feel it in herself. Mr Ringland had lived in her street for years, and it *was* true, the army drove about like mad things.

She couldn't believe that Mr Ringland was dead.

With a sharp little *clink* a stone hit the corrugated tin round the army base. Immediately an English voice appealed to the people to go home. Hazel got up on tiptoe to see if Sheffield was in the jeep at the front.

'He's not there,' Tina told her, 'you needn't be looking.'

A bottle cleared the high wire and smashed on a cement pillar. Instantly the soldiers backed away and boarded their jeep. Far out to her right Hazel saw two vanloads of policemen.

Abuse flew from the crowd.

'Get among the other side if you want to do some good.'

'Aye, they're the ones can scare you.'

'If you'd go and flatten some bloody terrorists.'

The jeep moved away suddenly. Now, a riot happened. Hazel did not see how it started or who started it: indeed it almost seemed as though the riot had started the people. Stones flew after the disappearing jeep and each time there was a hit, the crowd roared. On all sides Hazel saw faces shining with excitement in the white light. It wasn't normal.

Tina shouted: 'There's your Nino.' *Nino* was Colin's nickname. 'Look, he's away across the road with a whole lot of wee lads.'

Across the road lay the Catholic district. Sometimes it was the Catholics who came in their droves to stand and call their filth from their side of the road; sometimes, like tonight, it was the Protestants. Hazel had to fight for her balance as the crowd directed her feet where they didn't want to go. In a fit of claustrophobic fury she planted her feet firmly, twisted in the crowd, and broke away into open ground. Where Tina had got to, she had no idea.

By heading towards the waiting policemen she kept away from the worst of the jostling. The police stood talking in their long black coats, but didn't actually do anything. The front line of the crowd, where her fool of a brother was, had stopped on their own side of the road, and beyond, dimly, Hazel could make out the beginnings of a Catholic crowd.

Where had they all come from, and in minutes? How could so many people gather in such a short space of time?

Hazel was glad to find her mother in.

'I suppose you've heard about Mr Ringland?'

Her mother said wasn't it a shame, the army had only themselves to blame if any of them got hurt that night. Hazel didn't mention that she'd seen Colin, although Mum probably guessed that he'd be in the thick of it.

Her mother switched on the local late news. It was a peculiar thing, but her mum couldn't go to bed without hearing all the details about who'd been shot and where the latest bomb had gone off.

A while later her father came in, and Colin with him.

'Boys, there's fireworks up there tonight,' her father declared. 'Such a carry-on. Poor old Ringland.'

'It's a shame,' her mother agreed. 'He might have been drunk, of course. You know what he's like at the weekends.'

Hazel was as surprised as anybody when Colin reacted violently to his mother's statement. 'You don't know he was drunk! The Brits ran him down,' – he smashed a fist into his palm – 'just like that.'

Hazel winced. Colin sat sullenly in his chair. Her father lit a cigarette and her mother said, 'Tom, this is an awful place to live.'

*

Sometimes at the weekends, and less often during the week, the army ran a disco or a film-show for the teenagers of the area. Colin never went. He said it was the army trying to con people into thinking they were goodies in disguise.

It was at one of the film-shows that Hazel talked to Sheffield properly as he changed a reel. In his pale blue shirt, open at the neck and rolled up at the sleeves to show a bold tattoo on his forearm, he seemed very different from the person she'd seen with his rifle on the open street. He was still lovely, even though she hated tattoos.

He spoke first. ''Allo, I hoped you'd come. Where's your friend, then?'

Tina was at the club. Hazel said quickly, 'Why, what have you got against me?'

'Not a thing. I only mean you girls seem to do everything in pairs. Do you live round here?'

'Down the road.

'Number 27?'

Sheffield grinned slyly when Hazel laughed. 'You know about 27, then?'

Everybody knew about 27, where a woman and her daughter were supposed to entertain the soldiers.

'I live in the gable house.'

'And your name's Hazel,' he remembered. 'Nice name. Simple.'

Sheffield had to stay with the projector, so Hazel sat through two reels of the boring film with him beside her in the half-dark. At the end she talked to him while the hall cleared.

'I don't know your name yet.'

'It's a big secret.'

He was teasing her, but the soldiers had to be careful, for girls led them into traps sometimes.

'I suppose you miss your own people?' she asked.

'Not a lot. You have to fly the nest sometime, right? I get leave.'

'What do you really think of the people over here?'

Sheffield grinned. 'You lot are hard to understand, no doubt about that.'

'We're just the same as anybody else.'

He must have found this funny, for he laughed as he fiddled with the rewind switch on the projector. 'Listen, Hazel, if I was home . . .'

'In Sheffield.'

'. . . Yes. If I was in Sheffield I'd walk you back home.'

'Would you really?'

'Yes, really. Unless you didn't want me to, of course.'

'Certainly I would want you to.'

'That's it, then. We could go for a walk or maybe a drive in the car. If I did that over here . . .' Sheffield paused to make a clicking noise with his tongue, 'I might end up with a bullet in my head. Would you call that being like anybody else? You wouldn't say that was normal.'

Hazel had her answer for that, but he settled an arm round her shoulder and walked with her to the door as if he hadn't time to hear. The place was empty except for two or three soldiers in uniform, each with his rifle, and a group of people picking up tins of cola and crisp bags.

'I live in the gable house,' she said again. 'Call in for a cup of tea when you're flying by in your jeep.'

'OK, two lumps.'

'I mean it,' she said, surprising him into being serious.

'Me too, then. I mean it, too.'

She came down the road home wondering would he come, would she be in, would her mother be out? She was usually at work anyway.

The kitchen clock said eleven-fifteen when Hazel got home, so she spoke from the living-room door. 'I'm home.'

'Sounds like you want a prize,' her father said, and made her mother laugh. They sounded in a good mood.

'What would you say if I went out with a soldier?' she asked innocently.

'You're not! Are you?' said her mother sharply.

'No, I'm only asking.'

With half his mind on the television her father commented: 'It's a funny question to be asking. Gormless bloody roughnecks.'

'You don't have to be a villain to be a soldier.'

'No, but it helps.'

'Mummy used to go with a soldier.'

Her mother put a finger on her lips. 'We don't talk about it, love. It was before your daddy's time and it drives him mad with jealousy.'

Giggling, and ducking the cushion her father had flung, Hazel shut the door and went up the stairs. They wouldn't like her going with Sheffield. Definitely not.

At the top of the stairs she had to squeeze past Colin's home-made ladder into the roof-space. Funny, Colin usually pulled it up after him, for he liked his privacy. That was why he had nailed floorboards over the rafters and made himself a cosy little home-from-home under the roof. He even had a heater, the spoiled thing.

Hazel put one foot on the ladder and started up, holding her breath. She had never found it easy getting up there. In the days when her parents played Santa this was where they hid the toys.

On Colin's radio she could hear someone singing a country song. A bright bulb with no shade came into view, then the back of her brother's head. Hazel was about to say *Boo* when she saw the gun lying in his open palm.

Was it real? Oh God. Unless – this occurred to her as she crept back down the ladder – unless he'd carved it out of soap or something.

All over this neighbourhood, in letters a foot high from a can of spray-paint, you could see his nickname plastered on fences and walls, *Nino* this and *Nino* that, as if he were some kind of local legend. The gun was real. It was as real as Sheffield's rifle. Hazel felt sure there was something she should do, but couldn't see what.

Once more she saw Sheffield out on the street, and on that occasion she slipped him her photograph. Then two weeks went by without a glimpse of him. One or two times Hazel loitered near the base hoping for a sight of him, but that wasn't the kind of thing she could do too often without getting talked about at the club. Once, when feelings ran high against the army, a girl's hair had been cut down to her scalp because she went out with a soldier.

Maybe he'd gone back to England. Perhaps the answer was to forget about him completely. After all she hardly knew him. That was how she was thinking one lucky Tuesday morning – she was unwell and home from school – when she saw his patrol in her street.

Hazel could see the six soldiers clearly from the window. The patrol leader seemed to be pointing and directing as if he wanted them to make a search.

Sheffield came over willingly when he saw her waving from the side door. 'This is the house, then,' he said, approaching.

'Like I told you, with a gable. And you never came.'

'No wonder, I've had the 'flu. Been at death's door, I have. Hazel, where's 144a?'

'You have to go round the corner, it's a block of flats.'

'Right, I'll be back in a minute.'

Sheffield ran to the patrol leader with this information. Hazel saw him point down the road to her house and tap his chest.

'Pensioners live in those flats,' she told him when he came back. 'I hope the army's not torturing old people. Come on in.'

In his big boots and heavy warm uniform he looked out of place in the small kitchen, like an open umbrella or something. He said: 'We found a dog on its last legs, poor old blighter. It's a black Labrador. That's where the owner lives, 144a.'

'Poor thing. I hope it'll be OK. Would you like tea or coffee or something?'

He still carried the rifle in the crook of his left arm. A picture of Colin's ugly, blunt little gun came into her head.

'I haven't time. I could take a glass of milk if you can spare it.'

Hazel's hand betrayed her as she tried to pour the milk smoothly out of the bottle. As he drank, a crackling noise exploded from the lump in his jacket.

'No rest for the wicked,' he said, handing back the glass.

She knew what he was going to do, for his moment of hesitant shyness was shared by them both; but even so his encircling arm surprised her as he kissed her firmly on the mouth. The weight of him bent her spine over the rim of the sink, and while she was stuck there her hand crept round his back and made contact with the butt of his rifle. Then the radio crackled under both their chins and scared the wits out of her. Breathlessly Hazel broke away and Sheffield touched his lips, as if to adjust them before leaving. 'I have to go. I hope you didn't mind.'

'I didn't mind.'

'Hazel, you could come to the dance up in the barracks.'

She could not. Her mother said only trash went into the army camp for those dances.

'Let me write to you,' she said, leaning forward to touch her forehead on his shoulder. 'If I know how to write to you we can arrange to meet.'

'I'd like that.'

She spent a long time remembering what he'd said, every word, and hoped like mad that he didn't meet anybody at one of those dances.

When her mother came in, Hazel told her that the army had been round about Mr Arthur's Labrador, just in case anybody mentioned anything to her. Mum seemed to be in a state about Colin, though. When he got up to go out after tea, her mother told him in a voice she didn't often use: 'Stay where you are. You are not going anywhere this night!'

Colin remained standing, sullen, every inch the rebel.

'Tom, he's not to go out.'

Her father breathed deeply, as if breathing was a thing he did reluctantly. 'I don't know, I just don't know. What kind of a being are you, anyway?' He seemed more bewildered than angry. Colin just stood there.

Once started, her mother seemed unable to stop herself. 'I don't understand how you can do the things. What was the sense in it? Tell me, for I don't see any.'

Had they found out about the gun?

'You might as well have a ring in your nose,' her mother went on bitterly. 'For people can lead you anywhere.'

Colin flushed suddenly scarlet. 'Weren't they going to give his house to *Taigs*?'

Now Hazel understood. Over the weekend vandals had got in and destroyed Mr Ringland's house from the inside out.

'Who made *you* God Almighty round here?' her mother stood up to shout. 'You turned a good house into a pigsty, as if this whole place isn't a big enough sight as it is. Is that how you were brought up? To rip up floors and break windows and . . . You're the sort of a son who . . .

94

who . . .' Her mother gave up the struggle for words and brought her open palm across his face.

Her father lurched to his feet. 'Wait a minute! Wait, wait.'

With her mother turned almost to tears and Colin fuming in the chair, Hazel had her fingers in her mouth where her teeth tore at the flesh at the sides of her nails. The silence was worse, if anything.

'Look,' her father said to Colin. 'I understand all that, about who's getting the house. You think you're the only one looking after this neighbourhood? Andy Black had it arranged for squatters to come in and keep the Catholics out, but what do you do, you and these other two cowboys you knock about with? You have to do it the stupid way, like common criminals. Well I'm telling you this, boy. You'll be lucky to come out of this with your nose in the right shape.'

More composed now, her mother began lifting bits and pieces lying about the house. 'Oh I see,' she said. 'I got it wrong. Andy Black is God Almighty round here, not your son.'

The argument ended abruptly. Colin got up and came out with a rush of words like somebody beside himself. 'I believe in what I'm doing! At least I'm doing *something*!' Then he opened the back door, slamming it shut before they could stop him.

Hazel's father seemed bewildered and her mother spoke as if to someone far away. 'Dear God, this place will drive us mad.'

Why Sheffield? Why was he the one?

Five times she'd seen him now, each time longer than the one before but seeming shorter. His dad was an Al Jolson fan, they had an old dog called Lucky, his mum worked in a shopping mall the size of a cathedral, he longed to walk in space, his sister was at university and a brainbox, he was a radio ham with no interest whatever in football and she was doing her best to know him inside out.

Why not Alan, why was he not the one, with his handsome head and brown eyes and lovely crinkly hair that made you want to reach out and touch? Hair, eyes, teeth, shoulders – you could break Alan up into bits and admire every detail. She and Tina brightened many a dull period in school doing just that.

But not Sheffield. He was a lovely blur that came into her mind and made her feel good because he was there.

Hazel paused over her letter, pen in hand. How could she put it so that her feelings for Sheffield could be understood. She didn't think of him in bits. When she imagined him, the sum of him glowed. Glowing in her mind, Sheffield made her smile and smile.

And was all that 'love'?

She started writing again.

. . . I haven't posted it yet. I started it two days ago and I keep adding bits on. If I carry it round with me I get a nice feeling because I know it's going to be with you sooner than I am so I don't sort of post it. Does that sound silly?

I can't believe it, that you have only three weeks left of your tour. I don't see why they need you in Germany and I don't give a hoot about the British Army on the Rhine.

I've kept you a secret, Sheffield. I don't talk about you and I haven't

even shown Tina your photo. I pretend we're in a circle with strong
invisible walls and I'd like to keep them there so that they can't get
at us.

Yes yes yes I can see you on Thursday.

I love you. Hazel.

She had an envelope ready for it, already typed on a school typewriter. Hazel ran her tongue along the gum, stuck it shut, then placed it carefully in the pages of a history book. She lay down and switched off the table light.

About ten minutes later Colin came into her room like a beast from a dream, poison fangs dripping, and snapped on the light. At the top of his forehead his hair was matted with blood, and across her bedroom his breath told the tale of his drinking.

Hazel sat bolt upright. 'What *happened* to you?'

Colin pointed to his forehead. 'Over you!' He spat.

What was he on about? There seemed to be no sensible reason why he should be here.

'You think you're so damn clever,' he said, coming closer. 'You think you're so damn smart. You think . . .'

'What are you talking about?' she yelled at him.

'You've been seen, that's what I'm talking about. Caught out. Me, I'm the stupid one. I'm the one who doesn't believe it when they tell me my own sister likes the touch of a soldier's baton, that's what I'm talking about, you soldier's . . .'

She grew faint with rage that he should dare to come into her room and speak that way. But she couldn't answer him. Not yet.

'I'm warning you! Leave that Brit alone.'

Almost choking, thick in the throat, Hazel said, 'What business is it of yours?'

'I'm your brother, leave him alone!'

At that instant she loathed him. All the years of togetherness in growing were as nothing to her now. 'What'll you do if I don't? Shoot me?'

He pulled back from the bed, not so drunk that he missed what she'd said.

'I saw you with it!' she screeched at him. 'Up in the hole you crawl into. You're a big boy now, you've got something nobody answers back to, something you can run other people's lives with.' Hazel had been panting with the effort of spilling it all out, but now the words came easily. 'Well I've got news for you – *Nino*! – you're not running my life. You can bully Mum and Dad but I will sink you without trace if you try it out on me. Nobody round here is running my life. Nobody in this grip is running *my* life. Get out, get out, get away *out*!'

On the Thursday, Hazel caught the slow train to Lisburn, where she went out of the station on the high side and followed the main avenue through Wallace Park as far as the cricket ground. From some way off she saw him leaning idly on a pillar of the bandstand. Hazel didn't like to sneak up, with him being a soldier, so he was able to see her coming. Down on one knee he went, up there on the bandstand, with his hands on his heart and crooning away.

'I'd go a million miles,

for one of your smiles,

Maaaamee!'

'My father thinks he can sing, too,' she said, applauding. 'I think maybe it's a disease men have.'

He was easy company, Sheffield, not bored with what he was saying, with what she was saying. And not all the time obliging her to laugh. She found it deeply satisfying to be with him through the quiet morning.

After a while she asked him: 'Will you be glad to leave here?'

'No. Not now.'

'What about the stones and the spitting and all that – all the horrible things that could happen to you?'

'You get used to it.'

'I couldn't get used to people showing me all that hate.'

'Listen, Hazel,' Sheffield said. 'Every soldier in this army isn't breaking his neck to get out of the country. Some of the men with families actually want a longer tour of duty over here. Their kids are settled in good schools.'

She wondered what it was like living in married quarters. Perhaps his thoughts ran along the same lines, for he went on: 'The army wants me to do a course in radio communications. It would do me good when I come out of the army. I'm almost nineteen. I think about you all the time. I just want you to know that I could live over here.'

The park was almost empty. Hazel could see to the far edge of it, where a train came beating a rhythm out of Lisburn station. Under the bright sun of an April morning, this seemed such a peaceful place. A woman passed them, pushing a pram. She stopped to ease back the hood so that her baby could see a bit of the world.

'I should be at school,' she said.

'Schooldays are the best days of your life!' he informed the lowest branch of a beech tree.

'Then I might as well go hang myself,' giggled Hazel. 'I'll be eighteen soon, and you know what? Nobody ever said to me, Hazel it's great to be grown-up. Nobody over twenty-one has ever said it's great to have a smoke or a drink or have sex with your boyfriend. I'm not blaming them, mind, I dare say it's easy enough to wreck your life. Wouldn't it be nice, though, if they got a visiting speaker in just to say that the good times go on. It's not a case of death after twenty, is it?'

'You're a funny one,' he said, and kissed her sweetly. On the high side of the park, just out of the shade of the laurel bushes, Sheffield put down his coat for them to sit on. That was the day she first let him love her the way he wanted to.

Hazel left school in June with some exam grades to her name, and with a good qualification in typing. One morning late in the month her mother brought her the letter she'd been expecting. Hazel opened it with great care, for it was a letter she wanted to keep.

Dearest Hazel,

I've talked to my mum and dad about you and they want to meet you. Your letters are so wise and full of your own good nature that I wish I could show them to people to let them see what a great lad I must be if such a girl loves me. I should tell you the good news. I've been accepted for the course I was telling you about so we can talk about the future. Please come. My leave starts in the middle of July. I've sent you some money even though you said you'd not take it. If you come by plane I'll meet you. Of course, no matter what way you come I'll meet you and be over the moon to hold you in my arms again . . .

For most of the evening Hazel sat in the house by herself. Out there in the world somewhere her mother was explaining to her father that his daughter was in love with a British soldier and wanted to go to Sheffield to be with him for his leave.

She was going, no matter what. The reply was written.

When they came in, Hazel was ready. She was ready for the storm. Her father sat in the chair that the years had made his and never looked near her until he asked violently: 'Are you pregnant?'

'No,' she told him.

He began to untie the laces of his shoes, one of which almost hit the TV as he flicked them off his feet. 'If I'm to do my duty as a father, which I want to do, I'm telling you not to go.'

'Tom, let her speak.'

'What for? You're against it too, you needn't pretend. We haven't even seen him. God knows what he's like!'

She was determined not to lose her temper. 'Daddy, if I'd brought him here you'd have shut the door in his face and my brother would have spat in his face. You'd have hurt him as much as you could hurt without hitting him.'

'Aye! And I might have done that, an' all.'

He reached for the slippers Hazel had bought him at Christmas. 'Do you know where the British Army get their soldiers? I'll tell you where they get their fine soldiers. They go round the schools with a film and an officer and give a wee talk so's they can recruit the scum of the earth. The unemployed and the unemployable! That's how they do it.'

Like my brother, she thought. 'I love him,' she said.

'Love him! Jesus Christ! The ultimate excuse.' He swung his animated face away from her, as if to hear no more. Watching him stare into the fire, Hazel felt that he was near to tears as he did his talking to the coals. 'Years ago a helicopter goes over and the kids' eyes go out to here. It's something new. Now they wouldn't look up if the Brits landed on the roof. You gave your kids a pound and sent them off to the pictures or the football. It was a different world. There'll be a day of reckoning for that change, mark my words.'

'Daddy . . . —'

'Now what have I got? Now! Soldiers in my streets. Soldiers sticking their noses into my car. Soldiers through my pockets and now!' Her father's hand came up to cover his forehead and eyes. 'Oh God, now I've got soldiers tramping over my own flesh and blood, my whole, bloody whole life.'

The sight of him so distressed her that tears came to her eyes. 'Daddy . . .'

'I've said my piece, you can do what you like.' And he left the room without looking at either of them.

Hazel got her coat. Her mother followed her anxiously into the hall to find out where she was going. Hazel said she was taking a race up the road to post a letter to Sheffield.

I am gone into the fields
to take what this sweet hour yields.
Reflection, you may come tomorrow.

P B Shelley.

The Wraith of Bone Island

All things are taken from us and become
Portions and parcels of the dreadful past.

Alfred Lord Tennyson.

Austen was a nervous child with many fears about the world. He did not want to go to Bone Island, for Bone Island was the place where they buried people; but his mother pushed him into the boat and made him go.

When Austen and his mother had taken their seats, some men on the harbour wall lowered a long box into the stern of the burial ship. The box was made from the best of timber and sealed with tar.

'She's quiet the day,' Master Boyce called out to someone. 'Not a wrinkle in her!'

Austen wondered what he meant. He asked his mother and she said, 'He means the sea. It's very calm.'

'Hurry up and shake a leg, there!' Master Boyce called out to some stragglers. 'We want back before it gets dark.'

The thought of being on Bone Island after dark made Austen glad of his mother's arm around him; and glad, too, of the seals' heads lashed to the waling pieces. There was magic in seals' heads. They kept spirits away. Austen wasn't sure how, but everyone said that they did. 'Is he in that box?' he whispered to his mother.

'Yes, he's in the box.'

Until two days ago the man in the box had been his Uncle Ross who collected tolls from travellers through the high pass. An avalanche had crushed him in his wagon. Now Ross the Tallyman was dead and they were taking him to Bone Island to be with the other dead people. Austen wondered why.

'I don't want to go,' he said.

'Oh hush! There's Penn. Look at Penn, *she's* not afraid!'

Penn was his cousin. In many ways she fascinated Austen, for like many timid children he envied and admired those who did interesting things, even if they got into trouble. At this moment Penn sat on the box and it didn't seem to bother her that Uncle Ross lay inside it, dead. Actually she smiled at everyone who noticed her.

The boat began to move. Since this was a burial ship and a sail was not seemly, she had to be rowed. Austen watched seven pairs of oars slicing into the ocean together and listened to the deep chant of the hooded men, one of whom was his father. A strip of green weed on one of the oars reminded him curiously of hair. After twenty minutes, when Bone Island came into view across Blind Sound, Master Boyce made a special sign with his hands. This was to keep them all safe. Penn was the first to jump out when the boat hit the beach.

They dug a hole for Uncle Ross where the shore met the fringe of a straggly wood. The children were fetched to the front of the gathering so that they could see the lowering of the box.

'I didn't like him anyway,' Penn whispered to Austen. 'He wasn't my favourite person, you know.'

'Why not?'

'He said I made too much noise in his house, and I didn't.'

You probably did, thought Austen. 'But it's a pity all those rocks fell on him in the mountains.'

'Well, yes,' she agreed cheerfully. 'Come on, I don't want to watch them filling up that boring old hole.'

Hissing at Austen to follow her, she wandered off into the woods. Knowing that she would make fun of him if he didn't go, Austen went too.

Before long they had left the shore behind and arrived among some larger, broad-leaved trees which cast their shadows long and deep. Like a net falling, thought Austen, looking up.

'I bet they were pushed, you know,' Penn called out to him.

'What?'

'The rocks that smashed his wagon. He was probably giving some traveller a hard time over money.'

'I think we've gone far enough,' said Austen. 'What'll we do if we see the Wraith?'

'We'll just not look at it, silly.'

'It can make you look. It can make you do what it likes.'

'It has no bones,' said Penn. 'Did you know the Wraith has no bones? Not one bone in all its body. That's why it's all bendy and can change its shape like a puff of smoke. If it's got no bones, why is it living on a place called Bone Island? Isn't that stupid, Austen? Oh look! I've found a tiny little house.'

She had come upon a small beehive hut in a tangle of bracken. It had been built up in layers of flat stones narrowing at the top. Penn fell to her knees before the arch-shaped hole in the outer wall.

'Don't you go in there!' Austen shouted.

'I want to see inside.'

'No!' In the cold shade of the swaying trees, Austen had the powerful feeling that he knew more than she did about this place. 'Come out! The Wraith lives in there, I *know* he does.'

Alarmed by the authority in his voice, Penn stood up quickly and backed away. They heard voices calling from a long way off. As Austen ran towards them with Penn a step behind, he heard her giggling: 'Silly old Wraith, you've got no bones and you can't catch me, you can't catch me 'cause you've got no *bones* . . .'

How could she dare to say such things? Austen wondered. The Wraith had the power to strike you down with a withering sickness, or blindness, but Penn didn't seem to care.

The grown-ups were angry with them for wandering away. Austen's father and mother stood behind Master Boyce, who shook his fist at the two children.

'If you were bigger I would punish you both for your disobedience. Don't you understand? If ever you see the Wraith of Bone Island, let me tell you, you'll never have luck, never take fish, never have children, and you will grow old before your time. Get into the boat!'

Austen began to cry, but he noticed that his cousin Penn did not seem sorry at all. 'Rocks might fall on him, too,' she said in a whisper.

Now Master Boyce turned to his mother and father. 'Does he know the story?'

'Not in detail, Master,' said his father awkwardly. 'We thought . . . Well, he's young, still.'

'The younger the better! If he knew the story of Tai he wouldn't wander on Bone Island. Do your duty to the community, and tell him.'

His mother gave Master Boyce a quick nod and hustled him into the boat. The men rowed home without their hoods on, and Austen listened while his mother told him the story of Tai.

'Austen, once there was a time when a disease came among our people and many of our ancestors died. There were so many deaths that the bodies were not taken across Blind Sound singly, like your Uncle Ross today – instead they were ferried over in great numbers and just thrown into open pits. Those were bad times for everybody. You can guess what it must have been like.

'One of the bodies was little Tai. He was just a boy, very

thin. His parents thought he was dead and sent him over to Bone Island with the others. You see, they knew it was important to get rid of a diseased body as quickly as possible, for they had other children. It is important you understand that they were not bad people.

'As time went by, his father and mother thought they heard little Tai calling out to them. They heard him as one hears a child in the night, with an inner ear. "It is the wind," they said. "We cannot trust our ears, for Tai cannot be alive."

'But poor Tai *was* alive. And we know that he stayed on the island for a little while, perhaps some weeks, before his end came.'

'Did he live in a wee stone house?' asked Austen.

'I told you – nobody knows exactly.' His mother sounded impatient. 'Anyway, a spirit gave him the power to show himself after his death, and he appears to us now as the Wraith of Bone Island. We think he does work for the evil spirit, Shuaka.'

'Why?'

'Because the Wraith is always trying to get across Blind Sound to make us all sick.'

'Why does he want to make us sick?'

'Don't ask so many questions,' said his mother, 'that's just the way it is. If a boat is left over there without a seal's head, he comes to the mainland and brings fever. It is against our laws to fish near the island. You can't even collect seaweed for medicines or fertiliser from there, so you must promise never to go off alone on Bone Island again.'

Austen promised that he would not. 'But it was Penn's fault,' he said.

'Silly little goose. That Penn can make you do as she pleases.'

The boy Austen grew up to be a respected member of the community who lived on the Inlet of Bree. His family possessed neither land nor boat, and so, there being no easy way for him into the wealthy trades of farming, building and fishing, Austen practised medicine like his father before him.

The Healer Austen was an honest doctor, and a caring one. Specialising in compounds made from herbs and seaweeds, he became known for his unusual habit of keeping records of his patients and their problems. The walls of his cottage on the hill were covered with charts summarising the effects of his medicines; and he hid nothing. He noted those who got better from a particular treatment, and he noted those who did not. In this way, through attention to detail and a refusal to sell charms and false cures, he became a significant person on the Inlet of Bree. People said that the Healer Austen was a lover of Truth.

Many of his patients came from the more thoughtful population, who believed that he had a special understanding of childbirth. In time he sold his cottage with its tied-down thatch, and moved into the village of Bree. Not long after his marriage, his application for a permit to set bones was granted, even though this was opposed by the local quacks.

One day the Healer Austen was out walking when he saw an excited crowd gathered by the whipping-post at the centre of the village.

From the back ranks Austen saw a man lying on his face in the dirt. This was Penn's husband. The vicious ridges of congealed blood across his back bore witness to the fact that there had been a ceremonial flogging.

How he loathed in his heart that whipping-post, and everything that was done there in the name of justice! Elbowing through, Austen asked what the man had done.

'Been to Bone Island,' came the reply. 'Took eating crabs from off there, that's what he done. Put us all in danger for a pennyworth of profit.'

'Serve him right,' another voice said. 'He'll not go there again in a hurry.'

Penn herself arrived bearing a bucket of tepid salt water and a cloth. No sympathy came from the crowd as she gently bathed her husband's back. The Wraith, they feared, may have crossed Blind Sound in the man's dory. Soon it would flit from person to person, laying a fever on them.

It was frustrating for Austen to hear their ignorance, and to see how easily they accepted the need for cruelty. This was the kind of talk that had frightened him so much when he was a child.

'You can't stop disease by flogging people,' he said loudly. 'When we get sick it's not because of the Wraith.'

'You tell us why, then,' a voice challenged him.

'There are many reasons,' he replied. 'It has to do with being clean, with where we live, with what we eat and drink, with . . . many things. Some of them we don't know.'

'Aye. And happen the Wraith is one of them. It'll take more than you to tell us different.'

Had he known more, Austen would have said more, but he knew how true it was that there were more mysteries about life and death than he understood. One child died, the one next door got better. Who could explain why?

He knelt beside Penn. 'I have a lotion you can put on his wounds. It seems to help in such cases. I'm sorry about this, Penn.'

'You needn't be.' Fiercely, she wrung out the cloth. 'It's not the first time. I warned him they would find out. He had no business putting me and the children at risk. Well, now he can lie on his belly for a while.'

She stood up, tossing the cloth into a bucket. 'He didn't even take a seal's head. His boat had no protection when he came in at dawn this morning.'

'How did they find out?' asked Austen. 'I mean, was there some kind of trial?'

'I told them,' said Penn, gathering up the bucket. 'Send me the lotion and I'll pay for it.'

Everything about this incident shocked the Healer Austen deeply; but this revelation shocked him most. Penn, who had taken Bone Island so lightly, who had teased the Wraith for being boneless – that bold little Penn had grown into a woman who sent her husband to the whipping-post rather than face the Wraith.

Why did this happen? Austen, who sought always for the causes of things, could not explain it.

So the Healer Austen paid a day's and a night's hire for a small dory, and after preparing a satchel of food, and hanging a seal's head on an oarlock, he set sail for Bone Island.

Blind Sound stayed calm enough as he crossed it. A light easterly breeze had fetched over a massive sheet of low cloud so that Bone Island waited for him in a shroud of driven rain. The island was a raised streak in the ocean, the last known landmark to the north. The colonies of birds circling about the cliffs clearly had no fear of the Wraith. Neither have I, thought Austen. If it's still raining tonight I'll sleep under the boat.

By nightfall he had improvised a frail shelter at the edge of the wood. A modest fire he made there, which he fed with pieces of driftwood and brittle ribbons of seaweed. In the darkness Austen heard many sounds above the lap of the tide, but these were natural sounds. Sometimes the wind seemed to whisper as it shifted leaves. Waiting for the sky to lighten, he fell asleep and missed the dawn.

The new day was different. A mist had come down, greying everything, enclosing the local world within its damp coils. The very ocean seemed to have merged with it. Austen experienced a disagreeable feeling of confinement, and his heart seemed to tighten in his chest when he saw that the satchel of food had gone.

Birds, perhaps? Some forest animal? He stood up and shouted into the mist: 'I will believe what I see. Give me a sight of you and I will say, Yes – the Wraith is real!'

The mist was shifting before his eyes. And what, then, if he saw the unimaginable . . . ? How would he conduct himself if wisps of this creeping mist grew into coils and thicker coils, and became an insubstantial shape with eyes like burning coals? *Silly old Wraith*, he heard Penn say again, *you can't catch me, you've got no bones*. A clammy doubt seemed to make his blood run hot and shiver cold. Where could I hide? thought Austen. And he leaned on the dory, and waited for the mist, and Bone Island, and the myths of his childhood, to do their worst.

By mid-morning the mist had lifted so that he could see a watery sun. Half an hour of searching in the wood brought him to the place which Penn and he had found all those years ago. It was just possible, he thought, that the wretched boy in the story had built this beehive hut to hide himself away. Austen crawled in and sat in the little black hole that was such a monument to unreason. The Wraith lived, he had no doubt about that – but its host was in the minds of the living, created out of fear and guilt. What dark things we tell our children!

'Poor Tai,' he said aloud. 'No wonder you haunt us.'

When Austen returned to the Inlet of Bree in the afternoon, he spoke briefly to some fishermen and their wives who tended pots and nets on the pier.

'I have been to Bone Island,' he said. 'I brought nothing back with me, neither fish nor crab, and my boat was protected by a seal's head according to custom. I went there yesterday and stayed all night because I wanted to see the Wraith. I saw nothing because there is nothing to see. The Wraith is an idea, an idea without any truth. It stands in the way of progress and understanding.'

He was the Healer Austen, so they listened to what he had to say. Since none of them knew how to agree with him or disagree, his words were neither challenged nor condoned. The people drifted back to their houses and their work.

Soon, he knew, everyone would hear what he had done.

Months went by.

People still came to the Healer Austen, for his reputation had been great. The drop in numbers was scarcely noticeable at first, until one of his patients gave birth to a stillborn child.

Austen had to face the fact that people avoided him. They no longer called him over for a game of skittles in the harbour or tossed him a lobster with a laugh, and his conversations with people were stiff encounters confined to the weather and the price of vegetables.

'They're afraid of me,' he said to his wife one evening. 'Harald Wise, the stone dresser, crossed the road rather than bid me good morning! Why are they like this?'

'You know why,' said his wife.

'I went to the island, that's all.'

'You went to the island and your cousin Penn says it's the reason we have no children.'

'What does she know!' cried Austen. 'Are we the only couple without children in Bree? Anyway, I saw nothing, there's nothing to see.'

'Perhaps,' said his wife after a pause. 'But how do you know! Do we understand everything we see?'

As time went on Austen became less sure of what he had seen on the island. He still went for long walks to gather herbs for medicines – even though he knew he would never sell his compounds – and he would remind himself that *something* had removed his food during the night. And when that damp morning had dawned . . . how could he be sure that some vague Presence had not gone trailing by wrapped up in shades of grey?

He would return from his walks, muttering. People said, 'He is older. See how his hair is turning colour. He never used to carry a stick.'

Austen felt his loneliness keenly. It was a terrible force. One day, looking out over Blind Sound, he began to think about that mist again. Could it be that the spirit of Tai was so large an entity that it had enveloped him completely? He had not been looking *at*: he had been within.

'I have to go back,' he said to his wife, who nodded.

'I think you do.'

The fishing folk who saw his boat first tucked their blunt wooden needles into the mesh of their nets and sent word that the Healer Austen was returning.

People began to arrive in the harbour. A kind of excitement was brewing, akin to the kind that came with the landing of a big fish. Skittles were left standing under the pollarded trees as the players carried their mugs of beer into the tavern yard. Perhaps three parts of the population were present when Austen, smiling a little, came among them wearing a seal's head round his neck.

'I must admit to a mistake,' he said to the company. 'My thinking has been wrong about the Wraith.'

'You saw it, then?' The speaker was Penn's husband.

'I lit my fire on the beach,' said Austen. 'At the top, where the dry seaweed is. It came out of the woods.'

'Walking?' called a voice.

Austen smiled curiously. 'Drifting. It has no bones, as you may know. There was no form to it, what you would call a true shape. Its eyes seemed to blaze in the light from my fire – they had the glow of hot coals. It just hung there, I saw it plain.'

'What did it do?'

'Oh, it left me alone. I had a seal's head, after all. At one point I thought I might speak, but . . . I could think of nothing to say.'

They had many questions for him. It was pleasant to talk again, and have someone listen. He told them what they knew to be true, and restless children were smacked to make them listen. Then he walked home with his wife, linking arms on the way. She looked at him strangely, but asked him no questions about his visit to Bone Island, and he never spoke of it again.

Austen the Healer was patient in the months that followed, but eventually the people of Bree came to buy his potions and charms. If anything his work was easier now than it used to be, for he no longer kept records or took pains with troublesome details or charts. The people had faith, after all; they did not ask for proofs.

At this time Austen was thirty-two. He lived almost eighteen more years on the Inlet of Bree, which was considered a fair age. Late in life a healthy baby was born to him and his wife. They called her Shimna.

'The Healer Austen has a little autumn leaf,' the people said. 'See how thoroughly he has been forgiven.'

I have learned
To look on Nature, not as in the hour
Of thoughtless youth, but hearing oftentimes
The still, sad music of humanity.

William Wordsworth.

Blind Chance

There's a special providence in the fall of a sparrow.
If it be now, 't is not to come; if it be not to come,
it will be now.

William Shakespeare.

Jonathan Fane met the woman in the middle of the night as she wrestled with the serpent called Death. Her name was Miah.

The incident happened in a deserted Birmingham street (for it was two-thirty in the morning) when, on his way home from work, Fane saw an ambulance parked outside a house. An elderly man leaned out from an upstairs window, sobbing his breath away. Directly below him at street level, the front door of the house lay wide open to reveal a tunnel of light, within which Fane saw a hatstand and a picture of a stag.

Suddenly two people rushed up the long hall with a trolley between them. The young woman at the head of the trolley cursed as she stumbled slightly on the last step into the street. 'Why the hell don't they put *ramps* in these places?' Then she caressed the forehead of the old lady who lay on the trolley with a mask over her face.

The lettering in a glass pane above the door said Sheridan Fold. Although he passed this place regularly, Fane had not realised until now that it was some sort of sheltered accommodation for old people. The patient on the trolley suddenly tried to sit up, causing a halt to the swift progress to the ambulance.

'There now, you're OK. We'll soon have you right as rain,' the woman said, but she was frowning as she fiddled with a loose tube. Her face seemed so intense and full of care that Fane could almost believe he was seeing the face of an angel and his vicarious pride in her brought a lump to his throat. All the while the sobbing continued from above and a blue lamp flicked its intermittent light over the dramatic scene.

Fane felt a thrilling chill run down his spine, the way it used to do when he saw and heard a fire engine roaring up Prince William Road in Lisburn.

'Can I be of any help?' he asked, coming forward.

'Yes, just go away,' she said with the briefest of glances. 'There's always a crowd.' Then to her colleague she added, 'Let's get her on board.'

The ambulance with its blue light drove away, the hall lights went out, the sobbing stopped, and Fane found himself alone on the deserted pavement.

There hadn't been a crowd, he was thinking. He was the only one and she'd put him firmly in his place, which was fair enough – people under pressure didn't have time to be polite. For some moments he recalled the woman's energy and commitment, and remembered how two or three years ago, when he had done first aid in the Scouts, he used to run little silent movies in his head in which he rescued someone from drowning or applied the tourniquet that saved a precious life. Why did people say 'right as rain'? he wondered.

In the gutter he found a curled-up thing which turned out to be a stethoscope. Fane didn't know what to do with it, so he stuffed the various tubes into his coat pocket and brought it home.

The place that Fane called home was a flat with two rooms and a tiny loo. Returning to this place in the dead of night often made him think about the real home he'd left not so long ago. Home, *real* home, was virtually a physical presence with him. He could remember mundane smells and sights and sounds that now almost had the power to make him weep.

There had been tears in his father's eyes when Fane got on the ferry at Larne. He was leaving home at seventeen not on account of any great crisis, but because it felt like a natural thing to do now that he had finally quit school and had to make his way in the world. His parents explained to their friends that a relative had found him a job – he was going across the water 'to work in catering'.

'See you, Pop. I'll be in touch,' Fane had said, shaking hands, hoisting up his backpack, and his father nodded miserably. Fane knew that the old man did not blame him for leaving school early or for being unemployed. His father was not so much a blamer of people as a blamer of systems and a blamer of Fate. It was even possible, Fane reflected, that he was crying now because he blamed himself, as if he had failed to pass on to his son the genes that would make him a scientific genius or a snooker star.

His mother gave him a hug and a kiss. Fane loved his father more than his mother, although this was something he hoped his mother did not know.

From Birmingham he wrote to them about the job, wrote rather than phoned. He was an assistant in a small hotel, doing all kinds of jobs – porter, receptionist, cleaner of floors and windows and ashtrays, although he did not mention ugly chores like cleaning up sick in the lift. Oh yes, he had added in a postscript to the last letter, I'm taking a course in hotel management. He knew of the mysterious belief they had in 'qualifications'. Neither did he mention that the job often involved working nights or that he still had his dream of raising the money to put himself through drama college.

Now, before settling down with a glass of milk and a raspberry jam sandwich, he cleared a space on the table for the stethoscope. He had no idea whether it was fragile or virtually unbreakable, but there resided in the thing a kind of aura, as if it were a hallowed relic or an icon, and he felt obliged to treat it with care. Had that old woman died? he wondered.

Then he flicked through the channels, searching for something to watch for an hour or so. This was his routine on the nights when he worked late. As a rule, he rose around noon.

The following day when Fane called at Sheridan Fold, a plump lady in a uniform told him that the name of the woman he was looking for was Miah Wessam. 'You'd best not leave that gadget here, love. Try for her down at the Health Centre.'

Fane thanked her, and asked, 'Did the person who was sick last night get better?'

A shake of the head. The plump lady mouthed, 'Heart, love,' meaningfully.

'I'm sorry,' said Fane.

A receptionist at the Health Centre paged Miah Wessam, even though he didn't ask her to and he didn't particularly want her to. All of a sudden there she was, walking towards him.

'I'm sorry to disturb you,' Fane said, producing the stethoscope from a plastic bag. 'I think you dropped this outside Sheridan Fold last night. I was coming home from work when I saw you, that's how I happened to be there. Sometimes I work nights.'

'Join the club,' said Miah Wessam, taking the stethoscope to examine it.

'It's one of those things I haven't a clue about,' Fane went on. 'I mean, I don't know if it's worth twenty pounds or five hundred.'

'Much closer to the twenty. Yes, I remember you now. One of the paramedics said I was rude to you.'

Fane shrugged. 'People get in the way, you had work to do.'

'Well, this is indeed mine and it's very good of you to bring it back. You're Irish, I think.'

'Yes. Well, British too. I'm from the North.'

'Oh, the Ulster thing. You're a Loyalist.'

'Just a citizen of the UK. You wouldn't call somebody from Devon or Yorkshire a Loyalist.' Fane paused, not wanting to get into all that stuff. 'I'm sorry about the old lady who died.'

'Yes, of course.'

'You did what you could, though. It must be something special to have the kind of knowledge that saves lives. You were like that Greek who wrestled with the serpent, only he couldn't win because the serpent was Death.'

'Well, that's one way of looking at it,' she replied with a smile. 'I lose my stethoscope and my patient and you compare me to a Greek hero. Anyway, I thought it was Thor who wrestled with death. Isn't he a Scandinavian?'

'I haven't a baldy clue,' admitted Fane.

She was black. Well, not very black. This was an area of uncertainty for Fane – maybe Asian. Or Egyptian? He reflected that his ignorance would probably be offensive to her, but he had never known a coloured person. Fane grinned, thinking about his pop being an Orangeman.

'I guess I should go,' he said. 'It was nice talking to you. Good luck.'

'And you.' She waggled her fingers at him, then walked away down a green corridor. He found himself lingering to watch her slow walk, for lately the motion of a graceful woman disturbed him pleasurably. The high polished cheekbones, the dark eyes, the amazing smoothness of her forehead after the frown of last night – these were things he had noted and admired also; but, of course, he would never see her again.

Yet he did see her again. He saw her three weeks later, at the same early morning hour, in the same street and once more on a Thursday. This time the doors of the ambulance outside Sheridan Fold were already closed when Fane arrived. Some remnant of school learning reminded him that Thursday was Thor's day. These coincidences unsettled him slightly.

The ambulance left without her. From across the street he saw Miah Wessam framed in the yellow light of the hall, talking to two other silhouettes, trying to calm them down. When these others went inside, Fane crossed the road and spoke to her.

'Hello there. It's me again.'

There was no surprise in her face; she only nodded, leaned against the wall and said flatly, 'Life can be such a bitch.'

He wondered what had happened.

'You look out on your feet,' he said.

'Damn, I should have asked them to get me a taxi. Some of the old people are very upset. I had to stay with them.'

'I thought doctors had cars.'

'Yes, well, mine's in the garage, sick. A friend rushed me round here.'

'I'll get you a taxi,' said Fane. 'Come on, I live round the corner. Maybe I could fix you a coffee. Will you do that? Let me make you a coffee.'

'Lead on Macduff,' she said.

On the way Miah Wessam told him that there had been another death at Sheridan Fold, this time an old man of eighty-two. His wife had died three weeks ago to the day, almost to the hour. She had been the same age, eighty-two years old.

'That was the night I first saw you,' Fane remarked. 'Amazing coincidence.'

She said, 'Hmm.'

'I think I might have seen him too, at the upstairs window.'

In the flat she was very quiet while Fane phoned for a taxi and made some tea. He was glad that she preferred tea because he was not convinced that other people enjoyed his version of coffee. Each sat at one end of the rickety table he'd bought in a second-hand shop, a plate of biscuits between them. By good luck he was able to produce a carton of fresh milk.

'Tea OK?'

'Hmm. Tea's tea.'

'Was he . . . alive when you got there?' asked Fane.

'Oh yes. He talked to me.' She gave a laugh he could not explain, then slipped two fingers through the handle of a Dulux-dog mug. She was all of a piece, motionless. If she gave a start her whole body would jolt and the tea would spill. The more he watched her, the more certain he felt that she was not behaving normally. But he loved the stillness in her face and the fullness of her lips.

'Do you want a ginger biscuit?'

'No.'

'I'm a sucker for dunking ginger biscuits, but they melt if you don't time it right. Then you get this horrible mush at the bottom of the cup.'

'What am I doing here? This is completely bizarre.'

'Maybe because it's the night-time,' agreed Fane. 'I've noticed that things are different when everybody else is asleep. Sometimes I think it's a bit like being in the theatre. The first time you saw me you said, "There's always a crowd." You can only get a crowd of one at night-time. This doesn't make any sense to you, I suppose, but I just think that people are different by night.'

She seemed to be listening but her mind was elsewhere. Twice she had wrestled with death and she had lost and now on an impulse he took one of her hands in his, rocked it gently, then let it go. What gave him the right, or indeed the courage, to behave in this way, he had no idea. 'Are you going back to someone who will take care of you?'

'Three of us share a house. I think I heard the taxi. Will you be an angel and lend me ten pounds? I really did think I'd be going back with the ambulance.'

Fane leaned out of the window to wave at the taxi-driver in case he wakened the neighbourhood, then gave her two five pound notes, saying lightly, 'There you are, just call me Gabriel. The question is, what interest do I get on my loan?'

'Is Gabriel your name?'

'No, you said "be an angel". Gabriel's the big cheese among angels.'

'Oh, I see. And who is the angel of death?'

'Never met the guy. I'm no expert on angels.'

Now she gave a relaxed giggle, perhaps brought on by the absurdity of discussing angels at three o'clock in the morning. Before Miah Wessam left she gave him a piece of paper bearing her name, an address and the message: *IOU ten pounds plus interest, call tomorrow at two*.

When she had gone, something else of her remained in his flat: the smell of an angel who had wrestled with death and eaten curry.

The house where Miah Wessam lived was situated in a leafy cul-de-sac beside a public park. A nice little niche, thought Fane. Some of the trees soaring out of the pavement were almost as high as the houses. The bell in the front door was one of those annoying things that didn't seem to ring when he pressed it, but she opened the door almost immediately.

'Ah! *Entrez*,' she said in mock French.

'Mérci bucket,' replied Fane.

He followed her into a room where a huge couch strewn with cushions faced an electric fire set in a fake fireplace. Two wine bottles on the table had ugly collars of wax from the well-burned candles rammed into their necks. A bay window let in generous amounts of afternoon light, and in this light her hair was so black that it seemed radiant. How could that be? he wondered.

'You're staring at me as if I've shrunk,' she said.

'Sorry. I've always been a bit of a starer.'

'Anyway, I haven't thanked you properly for being so kind. So, what's your name?'

'Fane. Jonathan Fane.'

'Well, Jonathan Fane, I've got your money. *And* your interest, you'll be glad to hear.'

As she reached for the little dish on the mantelpiece, Miah Wessam's clothes became taut round her body and Fane longed to be close to her. Sooner or later there would come a time, a first time for him to make love to someone, and Fane had always suspected that he would have to be shown how, have to be guided through the process like a nervous and clumsy novice. Now he learned that this was not necessarily so, for the physical presence of a woman like Miah Wessam would empower him fully – had done so already even as he stood watching her. She turned and knew of his arousal. No stethoscope would she need to know the quickness in his heart.

'Can I say something?' Fane said, blushing. 'To me you're beautiful. That's why I was staring.'

A little grin; and then she said, 'You make it sound as though the rest of the world thinks I'm ugly.'

'No, they couldn't think that,' Fane rushed to say, the words tripping out. 'I've been thinking about the way we met. You know – that man dying at the same time as his wife. All those coincidences.'

'It wasn't a coincidence.'

'That's what I mean!' agreed Fane. 'Too many things happened together. After eighty-two years his heart and her heart stopped beating at the same time, on the same day and within three weeks.

But if it wasn't coincidence, then what was it?'

'What do *you* think it was?' she asked him quietly.

'I don't know. My pop says people are only straws in the wind. He believes in Fate. Things are meant to be.' Fane laughed, embarrassed. 'Maybe we were destined to meet, who knows?'

Miah Wessam came towards him and put the money into his breast pocket. 'I'm glad we did meet, you helped me at a difficult time.'

She was within reach of his arms now. 'It was a Thursday both times, remember?' he pointed out. 'And you were right, it was Thor who wrestled with Death. I checked it out. Think of all the things that had to happen! I mean, you have to admit it's strange. If you hadn't lost your stethoscope, if your car hadn't broken down . . .' He paused. 'Do you think I'll see you again?'

As if to admire the symmetry in the patterns of the rug beneath her feet, Miah Wessam dipped her head for some moments; then she spoke again with quiet deliberation.

'When I got there – to Sheridan Fold, I mean – Mr Conrad was very frightened. What happened wasn't a coincidence at all.' Her eyes flicked upwards, a single glance. 'Or destiny either. It wasn't a coincidence because he chose the moment. To him, that was the most natural time in the world for his life to finish.'

'I don't see what you mean.'

'He was married at twenty-one. They had been together for sixty-one years and he didn't want to live any more so he took tablets. It's as simple as that.'

'But he was alive when you got there.'

'Yes, he was.'

'You said you talked to him.'

'He wouldn't let me do anything, he begged me just to watch and be there. He talked to his Annie as if she was in the next room, waiting for him to come through and join him. Actually I couldn't bear it. He wouldn't even tell me what he'd taken and I told myself it was too late anyway . . . Maybe you were right when you said that things are different in the night.'

Once more Fane stared at her. 'You mean, you didn't do anything?'

'I held his hand.'

At that moment Fane had no idea what to say. Vaguely he was aware that somehow she had demolished the very idea of what he had imagined her to be. Nor did she help him. She only stared back. When the silence threatened to become ridiculous, he turned towards the door.

'Wait. Don't go without your interest!' So saying, she pressed upon him a packet of Gingernut biscuits. It was a small kindness, a continuation of his own little joke, and Fane acknowledged it with a half-smile; but once more he felt dismissed, a crowd of one.

Outside, kids were coming home from school. The autumn sun cast sharp-edged shadows in his path and he knew that she had allowed the old man to switch out his own light. *And who is the angel of death?* she had asked him.

Fane shoved the ginger biscuits deep into a pocket. An anger of sorts gripped him, but whether it was against her or himself or the blind chance that had brought them briefly together, he didn't truly know.

Riddle of destiny, who can show
What thy short visit meant, or know
What thy errand here below?

Charles Lamb.

A Matter of Time

As on the whirligig of time
We circle with the seasons.

Alfred Lord Tennyson.

John Dell was born in England long ago. His mum took in clothes for mending, while his dad – who was a carpenter – made scaffolding for the new cathedral.

John's dad used to talk about the new church to anyone who would listen. 'This will be the biggest thing you can imagine,' he often said. 'The spire will be taller than the highest tree – it'll make the bishop's pigeons dizzy to sit on it!'

'If they ever finish it,' said John's mother.

'Of course they'll finish it. It's only a matter of time.'

'That church was started twenty years before I was born,' his mother went on. 'And if you ask me, they'll be at it fifty years after I'm dead. And maybe more.'

When John Dell was old enough to walk, his dad often took him to see the men working on the church. He wondered what it felt like to make an important thing get bigger every day by piling up stones.

'Can I work on the church when I grow up?' he asked.

'Well, you might,' his father replied. 'Who knows?'

John's friends were Geoffrey Plante, Michael Carr and Catherine Lacey. They lived close to the market-place where people came to buy and sell.

There was always something to do in the market-place. You could watch the jugglers or chase a runaway pig; but what John liked to do best of all was to collect up the rubbish that people left behind at the end of the day. And then he built things.

Out of rubbish he built houses, towers, bridges, and castles for kings. It was hard for John to find enough rubbish to make all the grand shapes he imagined in his mind, but that wasn't his biggest problem. His biggest problem was Catherine Lacey.

Catherine Lacey liked to help John with his building, but she didn't know what to do. She would add an extra stone to the top of a tower, and the whole thing would go wobbly and topple over. One day she took out a mud brick to make a window, and everything collapsed in a heap.

134

'What did you do that for?' John shouted.

'I wanted to let in some light, that's all,' said Catherine. 'People need light, stupid! Are you building a house or a dungeon?'

'It's nothing now. It's just a heap of rubbish *now*, thanks to you! And don't call me stupid.'

'I will if it's true. And it's true, you are stupid.'

'Right, you're not helping me any more,' cried John, chasing her away.

But he couldn't keep her away. She used to sneak up and kick over his towers. One morning John built a great church which was almost big enough for him to crawl into. When he came back after lunch he found that Catherine Lacey had put half a dozen hens into it.

'Get those things out of my church!' he said.

'No. The hens love it in there, they told me so.'

John was speechless. He didn't quite know what to do. 'You can't put hens in a church! God is watching you, you know.'

'And you,' said Catherine. 'He doesn't like people who build a church that looks like a hen-house.'

At last John lost his temper. He wanted to rip Catherine Lacey's birch broom from her hands and use it to wipe the smile off her hateful face, but she'd be too quick for him. Instead he grabbed the hens and threw them squawking up the street.

'You cruel brute!' cried Catherine, swishing down the church with one mighty sweep of the broom.

As John chased her all the way home to Tanner's Lane he wondered how anybody with skinny legs like hers could run so fast. He found her on her doorstep, pretending to brush out straw. She knew she was safe now. In fact, she was singing.

'I wish you'd go and drown yourself!' John shouted at her.

She stuck out her tongue, and grinned.

Sometimes, in the summer evenings, John went into the market-place to watch plays about Bible stories, or listen to a storyteller describe the great elephant of Charlemagne. With Geoffrey and Michael he would enjoy the excitement of the hue and cry, and laugh when the priest shook his fist at drunk women dancing in the graveyard.

And just as often he would sit on his own, looking up at the church, worrying that they might finish it before he grew up.

He didn't think that they would finish it, though, because building was slow work. Now and then a war began, and some of the men had to become archers instead of builders. In the winter there was too much ice and snow to work. And, of course, there were accidents. Sometimes John saw men about the town who had been crippled by falling planks or stones, and these men made him realise that a great cathedral was not built cheaply. He often hoped that his own dad would never be hurt.

One evening as he sat thinking like this, Catherine Lacey skipped towards him. She was up to something, he could tell by the look in her eyes.

'The eel man is here,' she said. 'Let's go and see if we can scrounge a free one.'

The eel man sold living eels out of a barrel. He'd set up a stall in front of the inn and from here he shouted in a hoarse voice about the wonders of eel meat. It cleaned out your whole body if you ate it with chopped nettles and chives, and left the whites of your eyes clear in the morning.

'Ask him for a couple!' whispered Catherine. 'Go on, I dare you. Get one for you and one for me.'

'I don't know if I like eels,' said John.

'Now's your chance to find out. Ask him!'

But he didn't have the nerve. The eel man was a rough-looking sort in a leather apron, the kind who might give you a thick ear very quickly.

'I'll get one myself then, scaredy!' said Catherine.

She sauntered over to the barrel, and smiled up at the man as if she was a sweet little angel instead of a complete menace who wrecked things. After a few moments she came back clutching a wriggling thing half as long as her arm.

'Got one! Told you I would.'

'Where's mine?'

'You said you didn't like eels.'

'You wanted *me* to ask for *two*,' John shouted after her as she ran home.

After that, for a few weeks, Catherine's eyes lit up when she saw him, and she would yell out with glee, 'Hey, John Dell! Oh, you poor thing – you mean you haven't tasted lovely *eel meat* yet?'

When John Dell was ten his friend Geoffrey Plante ran away with some travelling people and Michael Carr fell ill with toothache. No one knew how to stop the poison spreading from his tooth, so he died.

That was also the year when John began to help a man called Matthew Walters to mend and thatch roofs. No matter how high the roof or how awkward it might be, Matthew could always get up there with his ropes and ladders. People used to call him 'Stickyfeet Walters'.

'Do you think you'll ever work on the roof of the church?' John asked him one morning.

'Me?' Matthew gave a rare grin. 'Aye, indeed, I'm ready for the church roof, boy – no better man! Except the church roof isn't ready for *me*.'

'My dad says it's only a matter of time.'

'Time! They've hardly finished the piers and buttresses yet. But don't you worry, I'll give them a hand all right when the time comes – if they can rise me up from six foot deep!'

On occasional days John met Catherine Lacey on her way home to Tanner's Lane, and he found that she wasn't half as mad as she used to be. The fact that she was working now had calmed her down a bit, John guessed. She helped a woman to gather and dry flowers, which meant walking in the fields for hours looking for suitable plants.

'What are these dried flowers *for*?' he asked her one morning in the bread queue. 'What do you do with them?'

'Lots of things,' she replied brightly. 'You could wear them in your hair, John Dell, and make yourself look gorgeous.'

'What else could I do with them?'

'Well, some of them are medicines, but they're mostly for that.' She gave his nose a tweak.

'You mean perfume?'

'Yes. You hang up a bunch and it makes a smelly room smell sweet.'

Catherine Lacey was as skinny as ever. She had dark, clean hair and John Dell thought it looked beautiful even without flowers in it. He smiled to think how she would be amazed if she could read his mind. And he liked the gleam in Catherine Lacey's half-closed eyes when she laughed out loud at the thought of a smelly room smelling sweet.

'What about you?' she asked. 'How do you like working with old Stickyfeet Walters, the human spider?'

'He teaches me things,' said John. 'We put some lead on the priest's house last week. Only, I'd rather work in stone, not lead or straw or wood.'

Slyly, Catherine glanced towards the cathedral. 'That's where you'd really like to be, isn't it? I know you, John Dell, you'd rather be up there building the biggest whopper of a thing ever seen in the whole world.'

'It'll hold a lot of hens when it's finished,' said John; and Catherine laughed again, as if she enjoyed the memory of the menace she used to be.

'Must go. It was nice talking to you, John Dell.'

Three winters went by.

One day in August John's father brought him to the cathedral. At the back of the church, work had started on the roof, for which the King himself had given sixty oak trees. Looking up at the strip of sky above the piers, John wondered whether even Matthew Walters with his sticky feet would dare to work so high above the ground.

His father approached with a short, powerful man who seemed to be all shoulders and no neck. This character peered close at John, as if he was looking at a calf for sale at the market.

'There's not much of you, boy, but you look sound enough. Are you afraid of hard work?'

'No, sir,' said John, glancing at his father. Who was this person with the strange accent and a face like a greasy pudding? What did he want?

'This is Ferdinand of Roquefort,' his father explained. 'He's taking on apprentices.'

That name on its own was enough to bring a rush of hot blood to John's cheeks. Ferdinand of Roquefort sat down with bishops, lords and princes to talk about stone. He had been brought over to supervise work on the cathedral after the last master mason had fallen to his death from a flying buttress.

'Will you teach me how to work with stone, sir?' John asked him.

'If you've got good hands and you're able to learn. Also, the quarries are in the hills to the north of here. You'll have to leave home, boy.'

Again John glanced at his father, who said, 'You'll find him willing enough, sir. The boy has always wanted to work in stone. I believe you'll find he has the gift for it.'

So it was arranged that John should go to the limestone quarries in the north. The night before he was due to leave home, there came a tap at the door. It was Catherine Lacey with a dish covered by a linen cloth.

'I brought you these,' she said.

'What are they?'

Catherine blushed as she removed the cloth. 'Nothing much. I heard you were leaving tomorrow. Just some eels.'

John Dell found that he could not look directly at Catherine. 'I'm going to the quarries. I'll be working blocks of stone as big as you are.'

'Mind you don't drop one on your toe,' she smiled.

'Thanks for the eels.'

'That's all right. Maybe you'll be rich one day, and have a horse and eat peacocks, John Dell!' After giving him a quick embrace, she was gone.

And when she had gone, John realised that there was something he should have said to Catherine Lacey: that he would miss her more than anything else when he left here. Yes. And he would rather eat chopped eels and chives with Catherine Lacey than feast on peacocks like a prince.

But the time had come for John Dell to learn how to dress and work stone. He spent many tough hours under the watchful eye of the master quarryman. With the sweat dripping from the end of his chin, or with the beginnings of an icicle at the end of his nose, he became the master of his tools. The great crude boulders from the quarry face, shaped by his hands, turned into blocks for the masons to build with. Each of these blocks he marked in three places: one mark to show the quarry it had come from; one to show the place it would occupy in the cathedral; and one to show who had made it.

His good friends among the stonecutters were William Norwich, who had been to the last Crusade as a soldier, and Thomas Walker, a boy of his own age. One day after sundown John said to them, 'Cutting stones is all very well, but I'd like to actually lay them finally in place.'

'Be a mason, you mean?' said Thomas.

'Yes. I'd like to put the stones right there with my own hands – be the one who makes the cathedral taller today than it was yesterday.'

'Me, I'd like to be the architect,' said William, tapping his head. 'I'd like to be the one who saw it all in here before they ever laid a stone or even *cut* a stone. The one who thought it up. Now there's a clever man!'

'Not any more,' John grinned. 'He died years ago.'

'So what? None of us is going to live to see this thing finished, you can bet on that. All the people who did the real work will be dead and gone.'

'If it's ever finished,' said Thomas. 'There's nobody working on it now because of the fever.'

'Fever?' John sat up. 'What fever?'

'You haven't heard? The whole town is down with a sickness. There isn't so much as the sound of a chisel to be heard in the whole place. They say even Roquefort has run away to Calais until the whole thing passes.'

Through all his growing days John Dell had heard many stories of fevers and plagues – the grown-ups talked about such things as often as they talked about the price of bread. He remembered the stories now, stories of so many deaths that people could not be buried separately; they were ferried by fever-cart to fever-pit, the inconvenient dead.

'But my family are in the town!' he cried. 'Everybody I know is there. Maybe they're all lying sick!'

Thomas, suddenly alarmed by the change in his friend, said, 'Well . . . They say it's not as bad as the last big fever.'

'Maybe it's worse! Maybe they're all dead.'

'Easy, John boy,' said William Norwich. 'If they're not too young or not too old they will probably come through. Just hope and pray for them.'

But hoping and praying were not enough. Before sunrise John Dell had already gathered up what food he could find for the journey home. A shadowy figure pushed a leather pouch into his hands.

'Some bread and cheese, that's all,' said William Norwich. 'Keep up your own strength what ever you do or you'll be no good to man or beast. I've seen the sickness in Marseilles and Rome, you'd be surprised how many pull through. How long will it take you on foot?'

'A day and a half, I think.'

'Good luck then.'

By nightfall he had come down through the foothills and the forests of the lower slopes into the plain, where he spent part of the night in a hayrick. By mid-morning he was already across the river, where the sight of the great cathedral rising above the walls of the town failed to lift his spirits. What was it for anyway? he thought bitterly – what use was that magnificent building when the fever came among the people in spite of it?

The streets were not completely empty. There will always be someone going somewhere with a cart full of corn, or wine or cheese; but no children ran in the streets, and traders who never missed a blink of daylight had their shutters closed at noon. John Dell hurried into Market Street.

'There's no rhyme or reason to it, boy,' his father said. 'Some catch it, some don't, some get over it as I did, many of them die. It feels like you're in a barrel of apples, wondering if you're the one who'll go bad next. They're saying the worst is over for the town and may God will it to be so; but that's no comfort to me. The damage has been done to me.'

He meant John's mother, who would never again sit in her cap, winding wool by the light of the window.

'What food are you eating, father?'

'I have enough food to do me.'

'What about the winter? It's warm weather now, but the first frosts could be here in six weeks.'

'Hah!' A tired flap of his father's hand dismissed the winter as a thing of no consequence.

John Dell didn't hurry down Tanner's Lane, and yet his heart raced as though Catherine Lacey had just knocked down his tower and he'd chased her all the way home. Had Death already paid a visit to this house in front of him?

Her mother, answering his knock, seemed well enough, but very thin. 'Mercy on us, it's William Dell's lad! Where have you come from?'

'I got permission to leave the quarries. Can I see Catherine please, Mrs Lacey?'

'She's been lying this three days. She gets no better and she gets no worse, thanks be to God. But come inside.'

The stale odours of warm, used air and dirty floor matting met his nose as he walked in. It would take more than a posy of dried flowers to make this smelly room smell sweet again, thought John as he gazed down at the figure on the low bed. Her face was turned to the wall.

'It's your friend John Dell to see you,' said her mother, settling on a stool by the window. The woman didn't have the strength to stand, never mind cook and clean.

Was she sleeping?

Catherine stirred as John lowered his weight on to the bed, and she spoke. 'You shouldn't have come. What if the fever goes from me into you?'

'Stonecutters are too tough,' he said lightly.

'My father was tough. Much good it did him.'

'Turn over, Catherine, and let me see you.'

'No! I don't want you to see me.' But then she did turn, and looked straight at him. 'You didn't think you would be met by this face, did you, John Dell?'

The eyes seemed huge and restless. Her hair was glued by her own sweat to the shape of her skull and red blotches swelled out of her face. This face, if she only knew it, was the dearest thing in the whole world to him now. He squeezed her hand and made her smile.

'You're the last person and the best person I ever expected to see,' she said.

'Well, I'll be back. I'll be here every day until you're well again,' he promised.

Life in the quarries had made a cook of John Dell as well as a stonecutter. In the evenings he prepared stews from the creatures his father snared in the fields or that he himself caught in the river. For breakfast he brought bread and broth, sometimes with cheese. And Catherine grew stronger. The blotches on her face hardened into scabs, and he had to slap her hands for picking them.

'When will I see you?' she said on the day he left. 'You have no idea, have you? It could be never!'

'I have to go back to the quarries.'

'Oh God, it will be never! How I hate the word. How far away are these quarries? You can come again, can't you?'

'Not very easily,' John said slowly, for he feared that it would be impossible. 'The same rules bind me as everybody else.'

'I'll always remember what you've done for us. I won't ever forget.'

'I had to pay you back for the eels,' he said, trying to joke his way through the emptiness of these awful moments. 'Just take care.'

On the way back to the quarries, John thought of a strange thing he had once seen. It was called writing. If only he could make those words, like lords and princes, he could lay out his thoughts and somehow send them to Catherine instead of his real presence.

146

This was only a passing thought. He could never make the magic of written-down words, and Catherine could never read them.

Some months later, Roquefort himself came on horseback to the quarries, looking for skilled workers. The winter frosts had passed and serious work was about to begin again. Among those he asked for by name was John Dell.

'Here is the situation, young man,' he explained. 'I lost some of my best masons in the fever last year. We're laying the webbing over the vaults and not everybody has a head for working up there in the clouds. If you're interested, come into town with the next load of stones and we'll get you started.'

In this way, John Dell came to live in the town once more, and to do the job he'd always dreamed of doing. Just as important as the new skills he learned was the ability to work as a trusted member of a small team, for it was a different world up there on the roof. One mistake could finish you. Or the man beside you. The masons and the carpenters and the mortar mixers didn't even come down for lunch. Sometimes John took his turn on the great wheel that lifted the stone blocks from the floor below.

May Day arrived. There were dancing bears and singing minstrels to coax the pennies from pockets. There were monks and nuns with their abbey wines; merchants from far away with silk to sell and spices to sell and pet monkeys, mother-of-pearl and feathers of flamingo. John Dell didn't have to spend a thing on entertainment – it was enough to stare at a heap of crabs for sale, or watch the crowd howl with fury when they suspected a pickpocket.

On this particular day he inspected the faces in the crowd as thoroughly as any stall, looking for one person; but he never saw Catherine Lacey.

Strangers now lived where she had lived in Tanner's Lane, and no one he spoke to had any idea where she might be. He could not bring himself to believe that the fever had claimed her after all.

And the summer went by. There was the winter to think of. One day as he stirred up a mixture of dung and straw – to smear on the new mortar in case of frost – a crowd of people surged on to the floor of the cathedral. It was market day, and they had been caught in a squall of hailstones. He saw a woman pluck a scarf from her head and flick her hair in the way he remembered so well.

'Catherine?'

He spoke her name – a small sound amid the bustle of the crowd and the din of men working. All the same, she turned towards him and walked forward.

'Oh, it is you! How are you, John Dell?'

'I feel well,' he lied. Perhaps she was promised to someone else, even married, In the name of mercy she might be a mother as well as a wife!

After a pause, for neither of them knew what to say, she glanced at the mix he was making. 'Don't tell me you're building a church out of dung and straw.'

He made no reply to this nonsense. 'I've been looking for you.

In every street, in every passing cart. I ask strangers if they know you!'

Catherine nodded. 'I gave up looking for you. I didn't know where to look.'

'But where did you go after Tanner's Lane?'

'With Mother. We went to live with some sort of uncle who turned out to be a bit more than an uncle, if you know what I mean.'

Some sort of uncle? What was she saying? 'You're not married Catherine?'

'Not *me*. Mother! You should see your face, John Dell.' She burst out laughing at the sight of him. 'He has orchards to the south of here. Sometimes I bring cider to the market for him.'

The hailstones had stopped. As they walked into the market-place he told her how he was working on the cathedral now.

'I suppose I always knew you would end up doing that. Maybe I'll come along and whack it down when you've finished. If I can find a big enough broom.'

'Will you come to the market again with your cider?'

'I will now.'

She looked at him directly – a look without any of her old cunning, just the plain truth. For the first time he dared to believe that they would be together.

Four carts on mighty wheels came crunching through the streets.

These carts, reinforced by struts and stays, and pulled by four oxen, were the main attraction in a procession of church people, and urchins in bare feet, and stray dogs and sellers of souvenirs, and a proud boy beating on a drum.

Four bronze bells were arriving at the cathedral. A light-hearted crowd had gathered to make the most of this free entertainment. John Dell stood among them with young William Dell, aged six, upon his shoulders.

The spire of the church had been completed by now; the bells were a celebration. More than eighty years after the laying of the first stone, the building had attained its full height.

It would go no higher, and yet so much remained to be done. John Dell was still laying stones on the front west tower.

He raised his eyes from the tumult of the procession to look again at this great shape in their midst – the most wonderful hen-house ever dreamed of.

What is it truly like? he thought. What can it be compared to?

He didn't know. For such a creation you needed men and their many skills; you needed wood and stone and metal tools and mortar and lead and glass – and yet it was more than all of these things. This church brought them together with such a deeply fundamental harmony that it seemed like a mighty chord sung out by all the workers of today and yesterday in their thousands.

There was something else you needed, and plenty of it: there was the matter of time.

'Daddy, can I work on the church when I grow up?' asked little William Dell.

How long would it last? John wondered. Could it stand for ever?

'Well you might,' he said to his son. 'Who knows?'

Only our love hath no decay;
This, no tomorrow hath, nor yesterday.

John Donne.

Quotations

Be good, sweet maid . . .
·from *A Farewell* by Charles Kingsley.

Then come and kiss me . . . (page 1)
from *Twelth Night* by William Shakespeare.

O, call back yesterday . . . (page 12)
from *Richard II* by William Shakespeare.

Now is the time . . . (page 13)
from *The Burning of the Leaves* by Laurence Binyon.

Time is the great physician (page 22)
from *Henrietta Temple*, Book VI, Chap 9 by Disraeli.

Sweet childish days . . . (page 23)

from *To a Butterfly* by William Wordsworth.

But at my back . . . (page 31)

from *To His Coy Mistress* by Andrew Marvell.

Thou art thy mother's glass . . . (page 32)

from *Sonnet III* by William Shakespeare.

Time wounds all heels (page 42)

Anon.

Time will run back . . . (page 43)

from *Hymn on the Morning of Christ's Nativity* by John Milton.

And pluck till time . . . (page 64)

from *The Song of Wandering Aengus* by W B Yeats.

Stands the church clock . . . (page 65)

from *The Old Vicarage, Grantchester* by Rupert Brooke.

That time may cease and midnight never come . . . (page 76)

from *Doctor Faustus* by Christopher Marlowe.

Ah! When will this long weary day have end . . . (page 77)

from *Epithalamion* by Edmund Spenser.

I am gone into the fields . . . (page 103)

from *To Jane: The Invitation* by P B Shelley.

All things are taken from us . . . (page 104)

from *The Lotus Eaters (I)* by Alfred Lord Tennyson.

I have learned . . . (page 118)

from *Tintern Abbey* by William Wordsworth.

There's a special providence . . . (page 119)

from *Hamlet* by William Shakespeare.

Riddle of destiny . . . (page 132)

from *On An Infant Daying As Soon As Born* by Charles Lamb.

As on the whirligig of time . . . (page 133)

from *Will Waterproof's Lyrical Monologue* by Alfred Lord Tennyson.

Only our love hath no decay . . . (page 151)

from *The Anniversary* by John Donne.